I0534861

The Boyfriend Bet

Sweet Snarky Romance Series, Volume 1

Chris Cannon

Published by CC Publishing, 2024.

Also by Chris Cannon

Going Down In Flames
Bridges Burned
Trial By Fire
Fanning The Flames
Burning Bright

Mysteries of Mystic Hills
Murder in Mystic Hills
Double Trouble in Mystic Hills
SpellBound in Mystic Hills

Sweet Snarky Romance Series
The Boyfriend Bet

Watch for more at https://www.chriscannonauthor.com/.

Dedication

This book is dedicated to my family for all their support. Especially to my husband for allowing me to freak out occasionally when the editing process makes me a bit crazy. And to all the fans who left ratings and reviews for Blackmail Boyfriend. You all are the reason this book exists.

Chapter One

Zoe

I sat on a bench in the quad waiting for my brother, who was late again. I shifted around trying to find a way to sit where my legs didn't come into contact with the lava hot granite. Whoever decided skirts were an essential part of the Wilton high school uniform should be throat-punched.

Where was Jack? I checked the Big Ben-type clock in the middle of the quad. As a junior transferring to the school, I had to attend Orientation. My brother, a senior, didn't even have to come today. Do you think he'd let me drive the car myself? No. He claimed he came to meet up with friends. I think he hates turning the car keys over to me. Too bad. I'd gotten my license last week and my grandma's old Honda Accord was now community property.

Someone sat to my right. When I looked to see who it was, someone sat to my left. I glanced back and forth between two hot guys wearing Wilton school jackets. One had dark hair, blue eyes, and a killer grin. The other had blond hair, brown eyes, and a serious expression. Given a choice, I would go with bachelor number one.

"Hello." I glanced back and forth between them. "Can I help you?"

The blond looked at a list he held in his right hand. "Ten bucks says you're Claire Barnes."

"No, I'm—"

"You're Deanna Case," the dark-haired boy said.

I shook my head.

"Lauren Tate?" the blond asked.

"No." What type of strange guessing game was this?

The dark-haired boy frowned at his paper. "You can't be Helga Svengack."

"You made that name up." I grabbed his list. No, it was real. Poor girl. I scanned the page listing the names of juniors transferring to Wilton Academy from private high schools. My name wasn't on the list. Probably because I'd come from public school.

1

"What do you think you're doing, Zoe?" My brother Jack stomped up to the bench, wearing his I want to punch someone face.

The dark haired boy gave me a look of disgust. "Please tell me you're not dating this loser."

"First off. *Ewww*. He's my brother. Second, he may be a jerk, but he's not a loser."

The blond flipped his piece of paper over. "You're Zoe Cain?"

I nodded. "And you are?"

"An asshole," my brother muttered.

The blond stood up. "Say that again, so I can hear you."

And my social life was about to go down the drain before it even started. Jumping up, I stood between them. "Can we dial back the testosterone please?"

Turning away from my brother, I held my hand out to the blond. "Zoe Cain, and you are?"

He glared at my brother for a moment before shaking my hand. "Aiden Eastman."

"And you?" I pointed at the dark-haired boy who seemed amused by the whole situation.

He sauntered forward, took my hand in his, and brought it to his mouth for a kiss, just like you see in those old movies. Totally corny. And I knew he did it to annoy my brother, but it still made my skin tingle. "Grant Evertide."

Holy crap. This was the guy who'd beaten my brother to become vice president of Student Council last year? The same guy my brother beat out for the lead in the school play? I gave him a nod of approval. "Well done. Very smooth."

He struck a pose and adjusted his green and blue striped tie. "Thank you. I try."

"Damn it, Grant. Stay away from my sister."

I pivoted around to glare at my brother. "He's joking. What's your problem?"

Jack shoved his finger in my face. "You can talk to any other guy at this school, but you are not allowed to talk to him."

Had my brother learned nothing in the last sixteen years? Apparently not, and for that he would pay. I turned back to the source of my brother's irritation.

"Grant, do you have a girlfriend who would mind if you kissed me to piss off my brother?"

In answer, he leaned down and pressed his mouth against mine. *Bam.* Instant heat.

I heard yelling, but I didn't care. It seemed natural to slide my hands up Grant's chest to rest at his shoulders. His arms went around my waist. We fit together perfectly. When the kiss ended, I felt pinned in place by the curious look in his ice blue eyes.

"Hot Tamales?" he asked.

And the spell was broken. I chuckled and backed up a step. "Close. Red Hots."

When I saw my brother's face red with rage, I laughed harder. He stomped off.

"That worked even better than I expected." I smiled at Grant and then ran to catch up with my brother, because I wouldn't put it past him to ditch me in the parking lot.

I hoped he'd give me the silent treatment on the ride home, but no such luck. He griped the entire time. We lived a good twenty minutes from campus, so that was saying something. Not that it mattered, I was used to him ranting about the things I did or the other injustices that seemed to happen to him on a regular basis, and I'd become skilled at tuning him out.

While he rambled on about how stupid I was, and what a jerk Grant was, I replayed the kiss in my head. While I had kissed a few boys, I must say this kiss ranked higher than the others. Would Grant want to kiss me again? I hoped so. And I'd do everything in my power to encourage him. The fact that it ticked Jack off was a bonus. That's what he got for trying to tell me how to live my life.

The Accord bumped up and down, which meant we'd reached the gravel drive to our house. From this distance, I could see my mom and grandma sitting on the front porch of our old farmhouse, shucking corn.

Jack parked on the side of the house in the shade of a giant oak tree, and got out of the car, still scowling at me. I ignored him and exited the vehicle before he launched into another list of things I couldn't or shouldn't do.

I climbed the weathered steps to the front porch, purposely stepping on warped areas that gave a little bounce and a creak of greeting. My grandma took one look at Jack's face and said, "Zoe Cain, what did you do?"

I placed my hand over my heart, pretending to be offended. "I merely demonstrated to my brother that he shouldn't tell me which boys I can and cannot talk to."

"She threw herself at Grant Evertide," Jack said. "It was disgusting."

"Oh, please. I did not throw myself at him. I asked him to kiss me to piss you off. There's a difference."

Grandma chuckled.

Mom shook her head. "One of these days you're going to cut off your nose to spite your face."

"Ignore her." Grandma patted the spot on the bench beside her. "Come tell me about this boy."

"You shouldn't encourage her drama queen ways." My mother ripped off a cornhusk and threw it in the wicker basket at her feet.

"Where do you think she gets her spunk from?" my grandmother asked.

I sat next to Grandma and relayed the story of how I met and kissed Grant. Her eyes twinkled. "Before I met your grandfather, I kissed Everett Evertide."

"Really? Then how did you meet Grandpa?"

"Well, Everett was a handsome boy and I always had fun when I was with him, but he wanted to kiss a lot of other girls, while your grandfather, God rest his soul, only wanted to kiss me."

"You're better off dating someone with a similar background," my mom said. "Your father and I had everything in common. That's why—" Her voice wavered and she sniffled.

A familiar ache blossomed in my chest and my eyes grew hot.

My mom cleared her throat. "I better start dinner." She stood and retreated into the house.

...

Grant

After Zoe left, I had a sudden craving for cinnamon rolls.

"You do realize Lena is going to hear about this." Aiden folded his list into exact fourths and slid it into his shirt pocket.

"Since she's my ex-girlfriend, I don't think it matters." Plus, I had a new and entertaining way to annoy Jack Cain. As far as I could see, it was a win-win situation.

"Have you told Lena she's your ex?" He pointed across the quad. "Because she doesn't look like an ex right now."

Lena stormed toward me in what I'd come to think of as tantrum mode. Right on cue, my head started to pound. Before she could start in, I held my hand out to signal she should stop. "I don't want to hear it. We broke up. You don't get to yell at me anymore."

Her eyes narrowed. "The joy of being your ex is I can yell at you whenever I want. I don't have to worry about you being mad and freezing me out. I can say that kissing some hick farm girl is low class and if you plan to go slumming, you should do it behind closed doors."

"The perk of being your ex is your opinion means nothing. Go annoy someone else." I hiked my backpack up on my shoulder and strode off, telling myself the wounded look in Lena's eyes shouldn't make me feel guilty. If she thought she was going to continue telling me what I should and shouldn't do after we'd broken up, she was dead wrong. I'd gotten off that ride and I did not plan to get back on. Relationships were not worth the trouble. From now on, I'd date who I wanted, when I wanted, no clingy girlfriends allowed.

"You know, this is why I hang around with you." Aiden fell into step beside me. "There's never a dull moment. You always do something entertaining."

A plan came to mind. "Speaking of entertaining, I bet Zoe has a friend."

"Statistically speaking, the odds are you're correct."

"Smart ass. I see an opportunity here for both of us to have a good time at Jack Cain's expense."

"I see this whole thing exploding spectacularly in your face." He smacked me on the shoulder as if to congratulate me.

"But you're still in." I knew the answer.

"Of course I am."

...

At dinner that evening, I sat across from my father as he read the paper. My mother stared off into space, sipping her third glass of white wine. Over the last few weeks this had become dinner as usual at the Evertide household. Cold, quiet, and calm. Unless I asked a question, no one spoke.

Tonight, my grandfather joined us for dinner, so I didn't have to carry the conversation.

"How'd your day go?" he asked.

"It was good." Remembering Zoe's laugh, I grinned.

"I recognize that look. Who is she?"

My grandfather could read me like a book. I cut a piece of steak while I considered how much to share. "She's new to the school, and she's the sister of someone I don't like, which makes things interesting."

My mom tuned into the conversation and set her wine glass down. "What happened to Lena?"

Was she joking? "We broke up two weeks ago."

"Don't worry." She reached over and patted my arm. "I'm sure you'll reconcile."

My father peeked around the edge of his paper. "Run while you have the chance."

My mom pursed her lips and gave my dad the I'm so disappointed in you look. "Yes, dear, because being involved with someone who loves you and wants to take care of you is a terrible thing."

"He's seventeen. That girl's mother has been talking wedding gowns for the last three months. She's insane. I repeat. Run while you can."

My knife hit the plate and made a screeching noise. "Wedding dresses?"

"It's what mothers do." My mom appeared flustered. "Besides, her family has that lovely beach house in San Francisco."

"We have a beach house in San Francisco," my dad said from behind his paper.

Mother sniffed and swirled her wine around in her glass. "Theirs is closer to the water."

"By a dozen feet," my father shot back.

Apparently this was not a new topic of conversation.

"Tell me about this young lady you met," my grandfather said.

"Her name is Zoe. She's impulsive and she laughs a lot."

"Sounds like a fun girl to date." My dad emphasized the last word.

"Zoe what?" Mom asked. Which is what everything came down to for her.

"Zoe Cain."

"I don't recognize the name. Did her family move to the area?" my dad asked.

And this was where it would hit the fan. Aiden and I had attended Wilton Academy since freshman year. There were always a few students who transferred in from other private schools, because their families relocated here to work for Wilton Genetics. It was the major employer in Canton, Illinois, and most of the town, including Wilton Academy, had sprung up around them.

The locals who lived on the farms scattered throughout the area didn't transfer over until junior year. That way their high school transcripts said they graduated from an exclusive private school, but they only paid half the tuition. We referred to them as hicks or farm kids. They called us snobs or geeks. Our parents were the scientists and lawyers that kept Wilton Genetics on the cutting edge of agricultural research and development.

The standard joke was that our parents were the best and the brightest in their fields while the hicks' parents were only smart enough to farm the fields. Our parents wore lab coats and created the genetically modified plants, which were faster growing, or more nutritious. Their parents wore overalls and drove the tractors. There was a weird White collar/Blue collar divide that was hard to get past. Sometimes the differences caused friction, like it had with Zoe's brother.

Keeping my voice neutral, I said, "Actually, she's local."

"She's a hick?" My mom's tone could've given someone frostbite.

My dad set his newspaper down. "Maybe you shouldn't date her."

"I dated a local girl when I was in school," my grandfather said in a wistful tone.

"What happened?" I'd never heard him speak of any woman but my grandmother.

"Life happened. We both met other people we were more suited for, so we went our separate ways. You're seventeen. Live a little. You have the rest of your life to worry about what other people think of you."

"I think I'll invite Lena and her mother over for dinner one night this week," my mother said.

"Then I'll be eating at Aiden's all week."

My father laughed. "I'm coming with you."

Chapter Two

Zoe

"I can't believe you did that." My best friend, Delia, skipped a stone across the pond on the back of our property. "Oh wait a minute. You are the reigning drama queen so, yes, I can."

"You know, I think a crown should come with that title."

"I'll bedazzle one for you. Now spill it."

"You should've seen the look on Jack's face."

"Yeah, because that's the highlight of the story." She plopped down on the grass and patted the area next to her. "Get to the good part."

I joined her on the ground, inhaling the scent of fresh cut grass. "It was the best kiss ever. I wasn't nervous. He wasn't nervous. It just happened like it was supposed to."

"So it wasn't like that time when Lee missed your lips and hit your chin?"

I cringed at the memory. "No. Nothing like that."

She leaned back on her elbows and stared up at the sky.

"Tell me about his friend."

"Cute, blond, brown eyes, serious expression, looks like he'll grow up to be a lawyer."

"I do love serious boys. They're so much fun to mess with. Maybe I'll tell him I'm thinking about starting a cult."

"You're evil."

"That's why we get along so well."

...

My alarm clock went off way too early the next day. The only good thing about being forced to wear a stupid blue and green plaid uniform was I didn't have to agonize over what to wear the first day of school. I touched my favorite pair of Levi's draped across the foot of my unmade bed. I planned to put them on the second I came home.

Next on the list, figure out what to do with my hair. For the past two years, I'd been growing it out, hoping to look like one of those actresses from a shampoo commercial. My hair hung past my shoulders down to my bra strap, but it sort of sat there, lifeless, brown, and in serious need of some highlights.

Maybe I'd have Jack stop at the drugstore on the way home so I could buy some hair color, and then I'd ask Delia to come over and work her magic. When I had tried highlighting my hair, it ended up looking like a kindergartener took a yellow marker to my head. When Delia did it, it was almost as good as the salon.

I grabbed my grandfather's watch from my jewelry box and ran my fingers over the inscription on the back: Time matters less than the people you spend it with. It was hard to believe he and my father had been gone for almost two years.

I secured the black leather band around my wrist, using the extra hole I made with a nail so that the watch would fit. It still hung a little loose, but that was okay because when I was nervous, I played with it like a worry ring, turning it around and around on my wrist.

It had stopped working a few months ago, but I still wore it every day. It made me feel like a part of him was still around. Funny that I found memories of my grandfather comforting, but memories of my father knocked the wind out of me. Maybe it was because I was still mad at him.

I checked the time on my cell, twisted my hair into a knot, and put on some bronze-green eyeliner which, according to a magazine article I'd read, was supposed to make my eyes look more blue. I wasn't sure if it worked, but it didn't make them look less blue. I added mascara and checked the results. Knowing I'd be attending school with girls who had unlimited budgets for makeup, hair, and shoes made my stomach hurt a little. At my former high school, everyone had worn the same type of jeans and shirts. There were a few girls who had gone all out with hair and makeup, but the majority hadn't.

Why was I worrying about this? I belonged at Wilton just as much as anyone else. And I knew I wouldn't be the only girl worrying about fitting in. My goal for the day was to keep things simple and blend in. I had no desire to make a name for myself, or be part of the popular crowd. I'd hang out with Delia, maybe make some new friends, nothing to worry about.

"Hurry up," Jack yelled from downstairs.

When we pulled into the parking lot at school, Jack cut the engine and cracked his knuckles. "I know you, Zoe. If I tell you to stay away from Grant, you'll go after him. Just remember, to him you're nothing but a hick."

Before I could return fire, he was out of the car. Fine. If he wanted to be a jerk, he could be. Why break an eighteen year streak?

I checked my schedule before heading for my first class. The last thing I wanted to do was start the day off by going to the wrong room. Small clusters of students stood around in the parking lot, and on the quad, checking for old friends, and eying up the competition.

As I navigated my way across the stretch of concrete, I played with my grandfather's watch, turning it in an endless circle. The cars were like a patchwork quilt of social class: BMW, Honda, Audi, Mercedes, Chevy, Acura, Ford. It's not like some of the farmers in the area didn't have money to buy high-end cars, but it was almost a source of pride that they didn't. The snobs seemed to want everyone to know just how much money they had by the cars they drove. As long as a car had four wheels and took me where I needed to go, it was good enough for me.

I stepped foot onto the quad and checked out the other students. Maybe it was the school uniforms, but unlike my other school, no one here looked like a slacker. How hard would I have to work to maintain my B plus average? I was smart, though I had to work for my grades. Math and English were easy but science classes put me to sleep. No matter how exciting the teachers tried to make it, I couldn't get into tectonic plates or the periodic table.

Since this was a small school, Delia and I would have most of our classes together. Lunch was a given since everyone ate at the same time. After coming from a public school where I could have been assigned one of three lunch periods, it was nice to know that worrying about who I'd eat lunch with on my first day wasn't an issue.

The random groups of students grew into a shuffling crowd the closer I came to the main entrance of the school. The buildings were beautiful, made of old brick and large blocks of granite. They looked like those Ivy League colleges I'd seen in movies and on television. The savory scent of coffee drifted through the air. I noticed several students holding insulated paper cups with lids. Was there a place on campus where you could buy coffee before class? That would be awesome.

Once I made it over the threshold, I checked room numbers. Even though I'd done a walk-through yesterday, along with all the other new students, it never hurt to be cautious. The last thing I wanted was to draw attention to myself by doing something stupid. My room, 107, was the fifth door on the left. Easy enough.

The seating chart on the chalkboard took care of figuring out where I'd sit. Unfortunately, there was a person seated between Delia and me. Since my last name started with a C and Delia's last name was Desmond, I'd hoped we'd be seated together, but some girl named Lena Clark sat between us. Hopefully, she'd be nice.

Students with coffee cups tossed them into a trashcan at the back of the room. The noise level in the hall increased. I, along with everyone else in the room, looked toward the door to see what the commotion was about. The most perfect girl in the world walked in. She had the perfect brunette ponytail. Perfect pink lips. Perfect curvy figure. Perfect unblemished skin. I stomped down my automatic hatred for her. It wasn't right to hate someone because you envied him or her, my grandmother always told me. I tried to live by that rule. But as a highlighting impaired, not-so-curvy female, it's not always easy.

When Miss Perfect checked the board for her name and came to sit behind me, I realized she must be Lena. Taking a deep breath, I turned to offer her a smile. She stared right through me. Of course my natural instinct was to cause a scene, so she'd have to pay attention to me, but I refrained. Despite what my mother thinks, I do have some self-control.

When Delia bounded into the room I laughed out loud. The school uniform must've stifled her artistic personality, because she'd added hot pink stripes to her chemically enhanced platinum blond hair. At this point I wasn't sure of her actual hair color, but the stripes matched her eyeliner, which made her brown eyes look huge.

"Cool new look. When did you do that?"

She tossed her backpack on her assigned seat and came to lean against Princess Perfect's desk. "Last night. I bought a box of blue. If you want, we can do yours tonight."

Miss Perfect snorted and made a comment under her breath.

I was beginning to think my grandma would be okay with me hating this girl. "Did you want to join our conversation?" I asked.

"No. I don't talk to hicks."

I'd never had this word thrown at me like it was an insult. I never thought it would bother me, but it must've, because the words that popped out of my mouth were, "Better a hick than a bitch."

"Congratulations, Zoe Cain. You win the first detention of the year," an authoritative voice said from the doorway.

Great. My face burned as I met the teacher's gaze, but I wasn't about to apologize. Instead, I nodded, turned around, and faced the front of the room. I ground my teeth together as I listened to everyone around me whisper. I knew one thing for sure, Miss Perfect was going down.

The next sixty minutes of class took longer than my entire sophomore year. When the tone signaling the end of the period played over the loudspeaker, Mr. Fletcher said, "The bell doesn't dismiss you. I dismiss you."

I hate when teachers say that. It sounds like they're playing God.

"Zoe Cain, please see me before you leave the room.

The rest of you are free to go."

Crap.

Delia signaled she'd wait for me in the hall. I trudged up to Mr. Fletcher's desk doing my best to appear respectful.

"Zoe, from the answers you gave during our discussion today, I can tell you have great potential. Don't let girls like Lena, or your temper, drag you down."

Okay, maybe he wasn't such a bad guy. "Where do I report for detention?"

"Come here. You can staple papers for me."

I escaped the room and found Delia waiting in the hall. She handed me a Hershey's kiss, part of the emergency chocolate stash she kept in her backpack.

"Thank you."

"Chocolate makes everything better." She bumped me with her hip. "Think about it this way. You're starting the school year with an I don't take crap from anyone reputation."

I half listened while the chocolate melted on my tongue, creating instant joy. Too soon, it was gone. I held my hand out, palm up. "One isn't going to cut it."

She dug out two more foil wrapped candies and passed them to me. "That's it. Unless you're bleeding, there's a three kiss limit."

"That's the strangest thing I've ever heard," a male voice said.

We glanced back. Aiden and Grant walked behind us.

"Hershey's kisses," Delia clarified.

"Oh." Aiden seemed to think about it. "That makes more sense." And then he pointed at Delia's hair. "Why did you do that?"

I interrupted before Delia could answer. "Delia, meet Aiden and Grant."

"Hey." Grant smiled at me and my anger over detention drifted away.

"You're right. He does look like a lawyer," Delia said.

"I look like a lawyer?" Grant sounded offended.

"No. Aiden does." I noticed the room number across the hall. "That's us. See you later."

...

For the next two hours, I played the model student. This was made easier by the fact that neither my second or third hour teachers seated us in alphabetical order. Lena sat near the windows, so I stayed by the door. Putting a little distance between us seemed like a good idea.

When the tone sounded for lunch, Delia and I escaped out onto the quad and headed over to the cafeteria. Unlike our previous cafeteria, it wasn't made of cinderblocks and it didn't smell like old grease. It looked and smelled like a restaurant, which served actual, edible food. That alone might be worth the cost of tuition. Plus the long rectangular room had windows lining three of the walls, letting in a ton of light.

"So where do we sit?" Delia asked.

Students had staked out about two thirds of the round tables with their backpacks or notebooks. "Let's grab our food first, and then we'll figure it out."

A boy walked by with three slices of pizza on his plate. Real pizza. Not the weird rectangular pizza they normally serve in school cafeterias.

"Pepperoni," Delia said.

"You read my mind."

Once we'd filled our plates, it was time to play, Pick a table.

Delia pointed to the single empty table near the windows. "Want to sit over there?"

All the tables by the windows were staked out except that one. Was there a reason it was empty? Grant and Aiden sat at a table across the room, which was already full. And it wasn't like they'd invited us to join them. I checked our other options. "Jack is over there. Let's swing by his table and ask him how this works."

My brother saw us coming and frowned.

"Don't worry, we're not coming to sit with you. I wanted to know if it mattered where we sat."

He pointed at the table by the windows. "Anyplace but there."

"Why?"

"Because teachers sit there."

"Good to know."

"No problem. Now go away."

"One more thing. I may be late getting to the car after school, because I have—"

"Detention." He actually smiled. "Good job. I think receiving a detention the first hour on first day is a new school record."

"Gee, maybe they'll give me a medal."

...

After lunch Delia headed to art class, while I went to Foods. The school required one creative elective a semester. Delia could draw almost anything, but she couldn't touch my coconut lime bars. I loved to bake and I'd been cooking dinner for my family since I was ten, so this class should be easy. There was a seventy to thirty percent ratio of girls to boys in the class. Most of the students sat at rectangular tables. A few loners stood off to the side. I recognized the where the heck am I supposed to sit expression on their faces, because I'm pretty sure it was the same one I wore. Why did everything in life seem to come down to figuring out where you belonged?

A pear shaped, gray haired woman entered the classroom and gave a grandmotherly smile. "My name is Ms. Ida. Everyone take a seat, please."

Crap. Decision time.

Grant stalked into the room, looking like he wanted to rip someone's head off. He approached the teacher and spoke to her in furtive whispers.

She patted him on the arm like he was a toddler. "Don't worry, dear. You'll love my class. Everyone does."

Lips pressed together in a thin line, Grant turned to face the class. I took a seat at a table with three open spots hoping he'd join me. When he sat next to me, I did a happy dance in my head.

"I can't believe I'm stuck in this stupid class." He leaned back in his chair and crossed his arms over his chest.

Someone was crabby. "For me, it this or art. I can't draw a recognizable stick figure, so here I am."

He leaned forward and spoke in a low voice. "I signed up for journalism, but some idiot overloaded the class. The teacher claims the guidance counselor checked all our schedules to see who would have to make the least changes in their schedule, and I was the lucky winner. If they'd gone by whose family made the largest contribution to Wilton Genetics, I wouldn't be here."

Okay. I was beginning to understand why my brother called Grant a jerk.

The girl to my left tapped me on the shoulder and passed me a stack of textbooks. I took the top book and passed the stack to Grant. He glared at the pile and shoved all of them to the girl on his right.

"You're supposed to take one," the girl said.

He didn't bother responding.

"All eyes up here, please." Ms. Ida stood in front of a white board. "Cooking is chemistry. If you understand what the components do, you can concoct wonderful creations. Man cannot live on carryout alone." She laughed like this was hilarious and didn't seem to care if anyone joined in. "Now, can anyone tell me what baking powder does?"

"It makes things rise," a girl answered.

"Yes it does. Baking soda releases carbon dioxide into the batter and acts as a leavening agent. For those of you who are wondering why you should care about this process." She stared straight at Grant. "Let me give an example." She removed the lid from a container on the desk and pulled out two cupcakes. One resembled a beach ball, which had lost most of its air. The other one was fat and round with a swirl of icing on top.

She replaced the cupcakes in the container, and then walked to the back of the room that was divided into tiny apartment sized kitchens. From a refrigerator she produced a metal tray covered in cupcakes.

"You don't have to take one if you don't want one, but I made these fresh this morning. It's a new recipe I'm experimenting with called praline cream." She carried the tray around and allowed each student at the table to take a cupcake. When she came to my table, the sweet caramel scent of the icing made my mouth water.

I grabbed the one with the most icing. "I think this is going to be my favorite class."

"Thank you. Since you have such a positive attitude, I'll partner you up with this young man." She inclined her head toward Grant.

"It's your lucky day," I told Grant.

He looked at me like I was nuts.

"Take a cupcake, dear. It might sweeten your disposition." Ms. Ida shoved the tray toward him.

He picked one off the tray and glared at me. While it was an impressive glare, I'd faced off with my brother for years, so it had little effect.

I leaned over and whispered, "I hate to tell you, but your fear me puny human look doesn't work on me."

The corners of his mouth turned up for a moment before he slammed them back down into an exaggerated scowl. "How about now?"

I pulled the wrapper off my cupcake. "Now you look like a Muppet."

Chapter Three

Grant

"I look like a ridiculous furry puppet. Is that what you're saying?"

Zoe nodded and took another bite of her cupcake.

It was all I could do not to laugh. She seemed so satisfied with herself. Her eyes were bright, her face flushed. If we were anywhere but class I would've given in to my instinct to kiss her. In the mean time, I'd plot revenge for that comment.

"Class, if you'll pair up with someone and come back to a kitchen, we're going to go over measuring ingredients. Do be sure to write your name on the bags of ingredients. You'll use them tomorrow to bake cupcakes."

"Are you going to eat that?" Zoe pointed at the cupcake Ms. Ida had forced on me.

Now that I knew she was interested, I grabbed the cupcake and studied it. "Not right now. I'm keeping it for later."

"You're just toying with me." She headed for one of the kitchen areas.

When I joined her she held up a spoon with writing on it. "Do you know what this is?"

I leaned in to read the markings. "It says tablespoon, so I think we can safely assume it's a tablespoon."

"Smart ass," she whispered so no one else could hear.

"Ask a stupid question, get a stupid answer." I picked up a smaller spoon and studied it. "They're all labeled. I don't know why people act like cooking is difficult."

Her eyes went wide, which could only mean one thing. Ms. Ida must be standing behind me, so I improvised. "If I can learn how to do this, I'm sure anyone can."

"I'm so glad you've come around." Ms. Ida patted my shoulder and then moved on to the next kitchen.

Zoe sidled closer. "I saved you. You should give me your cupcake."

"Wrong. You clued me in. I saved myself."

"Then you should give me half your cupcake."

"You already ate one cupcake."

"So?"

"So this one is mine."

"We'll see about that."

We took turns measuring out ingredients. It wasn't hard. Once we had the right amount of flour, sugar, and salt measured into Ziploc bags, I wrote our names on them with a navy blue sharpie.

While we were working, I noticed Zoe wore a man's watch. It looked old, and the hands weren't moving. "Cool watch."

She smiled. "Thanks. It was my grandfather's."

"Does it need a new battery?"

"No. It's supposed to be self-winding, but it stopped working a while ago."

"Then why do you wear it?"

"It reminds me of him."

"Time to clean up your areas." Ms. Ida walked around supervising. "We never leave a messy kitchen."

"Good thing she's never been to my house." Zoe wiped the counter down and tossed the paper towel in the trash. "Jack is legendary for making a huge mess and then claiming he has to go mow the lawn. One time, I left his dishes in the sink for three days. He still didn't clean them up."

"And what did you do?"

"I threw a new red tee shirt in the washer with his whites, on accident of course. Turned all his underwear pink." The evil grin on her face was contagious.

"Is it a constant war zone around your house?"

"No. There are moments of calm. My grandma is pretty good at keeping the peace."

"You live with your grandma?"

"My grandma and my mom. After my dad and grandpa passed away, she moved into the big house with us."

What did I say to that? I went with the obvious. "I'm sorry."

She nodded. "Thanks."

I tried to lighten the mood. "Big house? Isn't that what they call prisons in old movies?"

"My grandparents built themselves a smaller house on our property and gave the farm house to my mom and dad when my brother was born. Grandma said she didn't need all those bedrooms, so they built a two bedroom house out back."

"Sounds like you have your own compound."

"We have our own water, a generator, and a huge garden. When the zombie apocalypse comes, we'll be prepared."

"Yes, but you'll be stuck in the middle of a corn field with nothing to do."

Her eyes narrowed. "There's a ton of stuff to do. You can go fishing or swimming. What can you do at your house?"

"Watch TV, use the Internet, read."

"First off, there wouldn't be any electricity, so your TV and computer wouldn't work. Second, you think I don't have those things at my house? Why is that?"

And this fun conversation had taken a weird turn. "You do realize you're getting mad about a zombie apocalypse scenario."

The tone to dismiss class rang. She stomped over to her backpack and out the door.

I was beginning to think Zoe had anger management issues. I'd be better off staying away from her. Too bad. When she was sane, she was fun. I reached for my cupcake, but it was gone.

...

Zoe

How long would it take Grant to realize I'd stolen his cupcake? My next class was down the hall, so I leaned against the wall and waited for him to come find me. He appeared in the doorway a few seconds later, scanning the hall. There was something magnetic about him. It wasn't just the dark hair and blue eyes. Maybe it was the way the school jacket and shirt fit like they'd been tailor-made for him, while some of the other boys looked like kids trying on their big brother's clothes.

He spotted me, and stalked across the hall. I did my best to appear calm even though my nerves were going off like fireworks.

Giving a slow grin, I held out the half of the cupcake I hadn't eaten.

He stood there for a moment, looking at me like I was crazy.

"What? It's your half of the cupcake."

He snatched it from my hand. "Two questions. Do you steal food on a regular basis? And, were you really mad back there or was that just a cover so you could steal my cupcake?"

"First, I only took the half of the cupcake which was rightfully mine. Second. I don't plan ahead. I act on the spur of the moment. So yes, it ticked me off that you thought I was a farm girl who didn't have Internet, TV, and books, but I seized the opportunity to take my half of the cupcake while you were distracted."

"Okay." He took a bite of cupcake while he seemed to consider the situation. "I didn't mean you didn't have electricity. My dad loves his gadgets and can't bear to be without them, so we have backup battery storage on everything in the house, plus a generator."

Okay...now what? Time to confess. "I might be sensitive about people looking down on me because I started off the day with this Lena girl calling me a hick."

He stopped mid-chew, then hurried up and swallowed what was in his mouth. "You're the girl who called Lena a bitch?"

"I figured everybody knew the story by now."

"The story yes, but not your name."

The way he spoke about Lena made it sound like he knew her. "Are you friends with her?"

"God, no. She's my ex."

And my stomach hit the floor. He'd dated Miss Perfect. Well, of course he had. He was Mr. Perfect.

"Odds are she was mean to you because she's mad I kissed you yesterday. I think she wants us to get back together."

"And what do you want?" I held my breath waiting for an answer.

"I want her to sink her claws into a new guy and leave me alone. Maybe we should introduce her to your brother."

And I could breathe again. "Bad idea. I'd have to deal with her if she dated my brother." The halls were clearing out. "You better go."

The rest of the day flew by. Classes here didn't seem harder than the ones I had before. But there seemed to be more worksheets. While the worksheets weren't hard, they weren't much fun, either.

After the final bell, Delia walked me back to Mr. Fletcher's room. "Think Jack will remember you need a ride?"

"I hope so. It's a long walk."

"If he forgets, call me."

Delia and I didn't ride to school together, because she lived ten minutes in the opposite direction from Wilton. When she came to my house, there were back roads, which cut the drive to twenty minutes. But the main roads, which led to Wilton, took longer to travel.

"Thanks. Hopefully, I won't need to call."

She took off, and I went into Mr. Fletcher's room. He pointed at three stacks of paper each three inches high. "One from each pile and then staple. Three papers each. Got it?"

"Got it." I wanted to point out there were copy machines that stapled papers for you, but I didn't think that would get me out of detention. So, I sat and stapled until my hand was sore. Then I stapled some more. The good news is, the half an hour flew by. The bad news is, my hand resembled a claw by the time I finished.

When time was up, Mr. Fletcher waved me out the door. "Go. I'll see you tomorrow."

I bolted from the room and out the main entrance. Freedom. I took a deep breath of air, which still smelled like summer, but had a slight tinge of fall. Jack, who was supposed to be waiting in the parking lot, was nowhere to be seen. Neither was his car.

"You have got to be kidding me."

"Yep."

I jumped.

Jack laughed as he stepped into view. "I owed you after yesterday. Come on, I moved the car to a side lot."

"Jerk."

...

Jack drummed his fingers on the steering wheel as we drove to school the next day. A sure sign he had something to say which he knew wouldn't go over well.

"Spit it out." I turned in my seat to face him.

"Here's the thing. I know you think I'm telling you to stay away from Grant because he's a dick, which he is, but that's not the only reason. Guys like him might flirt with local girls. They might even go on a few dates with them, but they never take them to the big events. There's a fall dance coming up at school. I'm telling you straight up, Grant won't ask you."

And now I wanted to punch him. "Where do you get off—?"

He spoke over me. "I'm trying to warn you. Snobs don't date hicks."

In his own, obnoxious way, Jack was trying to protect me. "I get the message, but you need to work on your delivery. Because it sucks."

"It's not like you're ugly. Other guys might be interested, if you stopped hanging around Delia."

"Oh. My. God. Could you be more of a jerk if you tried?"

The last ten minutes of the ride was spent in stony silence. He'd barely put the car in park when I jumped out. Delia waved at me from a bench. I stalked across the parking lot, so mad I was surprised flames weren't shooting out of my nose. I joined her and opened my mouth to rant.

"This is for you." She held out a cup of coffee.

"You are the best friend ever." I sipped from the insulated cup and sighed.

"What did Jack say to tick you off this time?" she asked.

I gave her a brief overview of my conversation with my tact-impaired brother.

"Your brother is such a jerk."

I tracked Jack's progress from the car. He stopped and talked to several people who seemed happy to see him which was weird, since I avoided him as much as possible. Not that things had always been this way. Ever since the accident, he'd turned sort of angry at the world. I understood, because I was just as devastated by our dad's and grandfather's deaths as he was, but I didn't take it out on him.

"Do you think what Jack said is true?" Delia asked. "About guys like Aiden and Grant not dating girls like us?"

"I hope not, because that would suck." Not far from us, Grant and Aiden stood talking with two girls carrying designer backpacks. "Let's perform a little experiment. I'm almost done with my coffee, and there's a trashcan over there by Grant and Aiden. Let's see if they say, hello."

Delia held out her half full cup of coffee. "I'm not done."

"Then you don't have to throw yours away, but you're coming with me."

Delia knew arguing with me was a no-win situation. She'd learned this in kindergarten when she'd shoved me out of the chair I sat in because she wanted it. Of course, I shoved her right back and true friendship was born.

"Fine," Delia said. "I'll play along. Pretend I said something funny."

I laughed. As we approached the objects of our social experiment, Delia became more animated. When we came even with Aiden, he glanced over and stared at her. Then in an unexpected move, he stepped in front of her blocking her path.

"You never answered my question yesterday. Why did you put pink stripes in your hair?"

"You don't like it?"

"I'm not sure what to think of it." He reached out and touched a hot pink strand next to her face. "It's really your hair, isn't it?"

The girl who'd had Aiden's attention a moment ago shot death glares at Delia. And I was about to lose it and laugh out loud. Hoping to avoid an ugly scene, I continued on to the trashcan to toss my empty coffee cup.

On my return trip, I realized Grant hadn't made eye contact with me once. He kept touching the girl he was talking to. Nothing too obvious, but he brushed his fingertips across her shoulder and down her forearm in a familiar way, which I'm pretty sure is nonverbal guy language for, "I want to kiss you."

So, to recap, Aiden was touching Delia's hair. Grant was touching Miss Designer Backpack. No one was touching me. The up side of this experiment? It proved my brother wrong. Sort of. Just not in my favor.

A warning tone for first hour rang through the quad. I forced myself not to glance in Grant's direction as I joined Delia and we headed to class. As my brother had so tactlessly pointed out, while I wasn't likely to be courted by an agency hunting for the next top supermodel, I wasn't unattractive. I had modest curves, no different than most of the girls around me. I was average height.

There had to be someone on campus, besides Grant, who might want to ask me on a date.

Once we were in first hour, I ignored Lena and concentrated on not receiving another detention. She seemed content to ignore me until I passed her a set of the worksheets I'd stapled the night before.

"Grant didn't want a thing to do with you this morning," she chirped as she took the papers.

I took a deep breath and blew it out. It was best not to respond. Responding could lead to yelling, which could lead to another detention. At the end of class when we passed the papers back up to Mr. Fletcher, she smiled like she'd won a prize.

A spark went off in my brain. I smiled right back at her. "He told me he's done with you."

I heard her suck in a breath. I almost felt bad. But not quite.

At lunch, Delia and I snagged a table by the windows before lining up for food. When we returned from the buffet with our hamburgers and fries there were two other backpacks at our table.

"We've been invaded." I sat and reached for one of the backpacks.

"What are you doing?" Delia asked.

"I'm getting a piece of paper from my backpack to spit out my gum." I stated this like it was true rather than a complete fabrication. A quick check inside the backpack showed an assignment with Grant's name on it.

"Oh, this isn't my backpack." I feigned surprised. "This is Grant's backpack."

Delia laughed.

I opened my backpack and pretended to spit gum into a piece of paper.

"Why are you doing that?"

"Plausible deniability."

Grant and Aiden joined us at the table.

"Why were you looking in my backpack?" Grant asked.

"Sorry, I thought it was mine." I dragged a French fry through ketchup and popped it in my mouth waiting to see how he'd respond.

"Your backpack is blue." Grant pointed at the backpack in question hanging on the back of my chair.

"Today it's blue. I have a black backpack at home. So you can understand how I was confused."

Grant eyed me with suspicion. "I know you were up to something, but I'll forgive you if you have extra ketchup."

"Not that I'm confirming your suspicion, but here you go." I tossed him a packet of Heinz.

"Thanks." He ripped it open and squirted ketchup all over his fries like a red spider web. "Have any problems with Lena today?"

I didn't want him to think my life revolved around him, so I bent the truth. "Nope. She was quiet today."

"That's not like her. Once you piss her off, she normally fixates on the issue for weeks."

Great. "Maybe you're not that important to her anymore."

Aiden's eyes went wide, and then he laughed. Delia joined in.

Grant's eyes narrowed. He didn't seem to think it was funny.

"Don't mind him," Aiden said. "He's used to being the center of the universe."

Grant's expression changed from irritation to mock indignation. He sat up straight in his seat. "That's because the world rotates around me."

I heard someone walk up behind us, but figured they were planning on sitting at a table nearby. When the designer backpack girls Grant and Aiden had talked to this morning plopped down in chairs at our table, I had no idea what to say.

"This isn't where you sat yesterday." One of the girls complained. She moved her chair closer to Grant's, putting her back to me.

The other girl sat between Grant and Aiden. I could tell she wasn't the one who came up with this plan, because her face matched her strawberry blond hair. I decided to take pity on her. "Hello. My name's Zoe and this is Delia."

The strawberry blond nodded. "I'm Katrina, and that's Amber."

Amber stopped speaking to Grant and flicked her gaze toward us. "Hello. It's nice to meet you." Her words and her tone didn't match.

I hated fake people, so I jumped in with both feet. "Translated, that means, "Why are Grant and Aiden sitting here with you rather than fawning over us?"

Both boys laughed. Neither of the girls seemed to think it was funny.

The rest of lunch was spent in halted conversations between Aiden and Delia, and Grant and Amber. I sat back and watched the show. "It's kind of like watching a soap opera, isn't it?" I said to Katrina.

She chuckled. "This wasn't my idea."

I laughed, thinking she might not be all bad.

Chapter Four

Grant

Talking to Amber proved to be a mistake. She seemed to think she was auditioning for the part of my next girlfriend. I'd had enough of controlling females, and I wasn't interested in heading back down that road. I snuck a glance at Zoe, who was talking and laughing with Amber's friend, Katrina.

"Zoe, how did detention go last night?" I asked.

She grinned at me like she knew something I didn't. "It was fine. I stapled papers for Mr. Fletcher. Not a big deal."

Katrina sucked in a breath. "You're the girl who called Lena a bitch?"

Zoe shrugged. "It seemed like the thing to do at the time."

When I left the cafeteria, Amber stuck to me like glue. Lucky for me, her next class was in the opposite direction, so she had to leave. I caught up with Zoe and fell into step beside her.

She made a show of looking around me. "Lose your barnacle?"

I laughed. "Interesting description. Not inaccurate."

"Even I know the quickest way to make a guy run away is to throw yourself at him."

"But you threw yourself at me the other day."

Her mouth fell open and then she said, "Wrong. I used you to annoy my brother."

"Used me?"

She laughed as we rounded the corner and headed for Foods class. "You were convenient."

"Convenient?" I pretended to be offended.

"Pretty much."

"Is this some sort of reverse psychology? Because if I wanted to kiss you again, I'm one hundred percent sure you'd kiss me back."

"Keep telling yourself that."

We were twenty feet from the classroom door, but ten feet from a side hall, which led to the restrooms. And I wanted to wipe the all-knowing grin off her face. No teachers in the immediate area. What the hell?

When we came even with the side hall, I grabbed her hand and tugged her down the hall.

"What are you doing?"

Answering would take too long. I leaned in and pressed my mouth against hers. She froze for a second, and then she kissed me back. The noise from the hall faded away as she leaned into me.

"Mr. Evertide."

Damn. I stepped away from Zoe and turned to find the principal glaring at me.

"Sir?"

"Are public displays of affection allowed in this school?" His tone took condescending to a new level.

"No, sir. It won't happen again."

"To make sure it doesn't, you both have detention in my office after school. Now, get to class."

Zoe shot me a *this is all your fault* look and headed to class. I followed along, tempted to gloat, but figured it might be better to wait until she wasn't so angry.

Seconds after we took our seats, Ms. Ida launched into a speech about the different kinds of vanilla. Not that I cared, but I pretended to be fascinated to avoid eye contact with Zoe.

"All right, class. Back to the kitchens to start mixing your cupcakes."

Jumping out of her seat, Zoe made it to the kitchen before me and started sorting ingredients on the countertop. I strolled back to meet her.

She met my gaze and laughed. "Don't you look pleased with yourself."

"Because I was right." I leaned in like I was checking out the recipe on the countertop and whispered in her ear, "One hundred percent right."

A quick inhalation from Zoe meant what? Anger?

Irritation?

She retrieved a large mixing bowl from one of the cabinets. Grabbing our Ziploc bags full of ingredients, she dumped their contents in the bowl.

"Yes, and you are one hundred percent giving me a ride home from detention, because my brother has to work tonight."

That was not part of my plan. "I don't—"

She bumped me with her hip, knocking me off balance.

"Wrong answer. Try again." I caught myself on the counter.

"You brought this on yourself." She shoved the bowl at me. "Stir this while I crack the eggs."

"You're bossy."

"I prefer to think of myself as confident."

Why did I suddenly feel like she'd manipulated this entire situation?

...

Zoe

I'll admit it, I had teased Grant, hoping he'd kiss me to prove me wrong. But I'd meant for him to kiss me after school, not in the hallway in front of the principal so I'd have detention, again. It was hard to be mad now, though, especially since he'd be giving me a ride home tonight. I couldn't have planned this better if I tried.

Was there any way I could convince him we needed to stop and have pizza on the way home? Probably not. I could, however, accidentally leave one of my earrings in his car, which would give me a reason to talk to him tomorrow.

There. I had a plan.

"What's next?" he asked.

At first I thought he was talking about the earring plan. Then I realized he meant the cake batter. I read the recipe. "Crap. We should have preheated the oven."

"The ovens are still on from the last class, but you should remember to check next time," Ms. Ida said.

"We will." She sidled off to sneak up on some other unsuspecting students. I elbowed Grant. "What kind of ninja shoes is she wearing?"

"Ninja shoes?"

"You know, quiet like a ninja, and able to sneak up on people."

"No, I got it. It's just a weird thing to say."

I threw the wax paper cupcake liners at him. Catching them, he turned them over examining them from all sides. "This is what we put the batter in?"

"No." I grabbed the cupcake pan from the drying rack. "Those are the liners you put in the pan. Haven't you ever made cupcakes?"

"Why would I make cupcakes when there are bakeries?"

No way. "You've never made cupcakes with your mom? Or watched her bake them?"

He laughed. "I'm not sure my mother knows how to turn on the stove."

My mind boggled. "No baking cookies and eating them warm from the oven?"

He shook his head.

"Not even the slice and bake kind?"

"What's the big deal?"

"That's just wrong." So many of my warm family memories came from baking with my mom and grandma: fresh peach pie, birthday cakes, Christmas cookies. I grabbed the cupcake liners from him and started filling the pan.

"You've led a sad life."

"You're joking, right?"

"No. If you've never had chocolate chip cookies hot from the oven when the chocolate is all melted and gooey, then you've missed out." I checked the drawers and found an ice cream scoop to ladle the batter into the pan.

"What are you doing with that?"

I demonstrated how to scoop the batter into the cupcake tin. "Here, give it a shot."

"Because otherwise I'll be sad?"

"Smart ass." I mouthed the words in case our ninja teacher was sneaking up behind me.

Once the cupcakes were in the oven, I took off my grandfather's watch and tucked it in my pocket, grabbed the dish soap, and filled one side of the sink with hot water.

"I thought we were done." Grant edged away from our kitchen.

"Do you think dishes clean themselves?" I tossed him a towel so he could dry.

"They do at my house," he muttered.

The sweet scent of vanilla filled the air. I inhaled and my mouth watered. "I wish we were eating these today."

"We're not?"

"They'll finish cooking, but then they'll need time to cool. And we still have to make the icing. No eating until tomorrow." I washed the mixing bowl and held it out to him.

He pretended not to notice.

"You can dry it or you can wear it as a hat."

"Or you could dry it. You seem to be doing so well—"

Standing on tiptoe, I made a half-hearted attempt to put the upside-down bowl on his head.

He snatched it from my hand. "Did you really think that would work?"

"It was worth a try." Plus it accomplished what I wanted—the bowl was in his hands now, so he could dry it.

Should I gloat? Probably not.

Parting ways with him when class ended sucked. Whenever he paid attention to me warm sunshine filled my chest. Not that it meant anything, but it was nice to have a guy like Grant notice me. In a weird way, it sort of validated that I belonged at Wilton. And yes, that was some messed up logic, but that's how I felt. Not that I'd admit it to anyone, not even Delia.

Lena must've heard about the kiss, because in my next class she glared at me like she was trying to set my hair on fire with her mind. Was I surprised she'd heard about it already? Not really. Rumors are the currency of any high school. Come up with a good one and your status is elevated. Ten minutes after I received detention, I bet the entire school heard about it. And it did seem like the entire student body had heard about it.

What was the big deal? Why were boys I didn't know snickering and muttering under their breath when I passed them in the hall? It was a kiss. I even overheard a few boys say something about a ring. Did they think Grant had given me a ring? Grant wore a class ring. I'd seen it on his hand. Did they think I kissed Grant because he asked me to be his girlfriend? That would be a little stalker-ish at this point, since we'd just met a few days ago.

My brother cornered me after school, looking like he'd spit fire when he opened his mouth to speak. "You're an idiot."

Oh, good. No flames. Just the usual insults. "And you're a jerk."

He stepped closer, invading my personal space. I hated it when he used his height to loom over me when we argued. "Zoe, how can you be so stupid? I told you—"

"You're not in charge of my life." I whipped my backpack off my shoulder and around to my front, holding it like a shield. "Go away, Jack."

"Fine. I work tonight, so you better hope Delia can give you a ride home. It's a long walk."

"Grant is giving me a ride."

He backed up a step, like I'd shocked him. Eyes narrowed, he marched off to bestow his fabulous personality on someone else.

Delia ran up to me a moment later. "I expect a full report when you get home." She wiggled her eyebrows. "Make sure you have something interesting to share."

I laughed and headed to the principal's office where the secretary directed me to sit at a table in the back corner of the office. "Be quiet, do your homework, and you can leave when the timer goes off." She pulled a chicken-shaped kitchen timer from her desk drawer, twisted the bird's head a quarter of the way around and went back to her paperwork.

Whoever made those timers had a sick sense of humor.

Grant showed up with a frown on his face.

"What's wrong?"

"Your brother is an asshole."

"No argument there." I opened my history text book.

"What did he do?"

"He accused me of something." Grant pressed his lips together in a thin line and checked to make sure the secretary wasn't paying attention to us. "What he said...I'm not doing that."

Okay. "There was a big chunk of information missing in that explanation."

"No talking," the secretary called out.

Her timing sucked. What wasn't Grant doing? Minutes dragged by. Did my brother accuse him of using me? Was that it? It was a kiss, for heaven's sake. If Jack's interference messed this up for me I would kill him, slowly, by poisoning his food.

By the time the secretary dismissed us I was crazy with curiosity. We were two feet from the office when I cracked. "What aren't you doing?"

"I'm parked in the side lot." He kept walking like he hadn't heard me.

"That wasn't an answer." Keeping up with his longer stride meant doing an awkward half run. "And you need to slow down."

He didn't answer me, but he did slow down. A small victory.

"We'll talk in the car."

Did he think the hallways were bugged? "There's no one here." I gestured to the empty space around us.

"Trust me. When I fill you in, you're going to be mad. And we've already established that you're not quiet when you're angry."

That warm feeling I normally had around him changed into a bucket of ice water dumped on my head. "Angry at my brother or angry at you?"

"I'm innocent in this." We exited the building and I shivered. Whether it was due to the cool autumn air or the upcoming reveal, I wasn't sure.

Grant pulled out his keys and pressed a button. An ink black sports car beeped and flashed its lights.

"Cute car."

He stopped mid-stride. "Cute?"

The appalled expression on his face had me clamping my lips together to keep from laughing. I held my hands up in surrender and took a steadying breath. "Sorry. Let me try again. My, what a masculine, studly car you have. Better?"

"Much better." He held his fingers out like he was measuring something two inches long. "You were this close to walking home."

I laughed. The earlier tension faded away. When we reached the car, he opened the door for me. The seat seemed lower than normal. And I was wearing a skirt. Solution? Awkward squat while praying I didn't flash Grant. Reality? Skirt sliding halfway up my thighs, but thankfully my lime green underwear with day-glow yellow hearts, which I'd purchased off the clearance table, remained a secret. Note to self, buy sexy or at least non-embarrassing underwear.

During the time he walked around the car and climbed in, I adjusted my skirt to provide respectable coverage.

"Which way is home?" Grant started the car, which roared like a lion. The vibrations from the engine rattled my teeth. I don't understand why guys think that's cool.

"Out Highway Twenty and then a left on Bakersfield Road."

We were out of the parking lot and onto the highway in seconds. "Tell me when we're close to the turn off. I've never been out this way."

The little voice in my head urged me to continue our earlier conversation. But right now, there was a happy calm between us, and I didn't want to let that go. "We'll hit the turn off in about ten minutes."

"How long until we reach your zombie apocalypse safe compound?" The teasing tone of his voice made me laugh.

"About ten minutes after that." I relaxed back in the soft leather seat, wanting to forget about whatever my brother had accused Grant of, but it was like an irritating pebble in my shoe—impossible to ignore. "Are you going to tell me what happened with my brother?"

"No matter what I say, you'll end up pissed off." He tapped his fingers on the steering wheel. "Have you heard the term, ringer?"

"Like when you're throwing horseshoes?"

"No. It's short for dead ringer, like a copycat. Every year, there are a few guys who have a competition to see who can get a hick—I mean a local girl—to fall for them. Once they hook up, the guy breaks things off because she's not someone he wants for a real girlfriend. She's a ringer."

Volcanic rage erupted inside me. I took a deep breath so I wouldn't spew lava all over Grant. "They have a competition? Any guy who does that should be neutered with hedge clippers."

Click. My brain made the connection and my mouth went dry. The snickering boys muttering about rings. No not about rings, ringers. They were calling me a ringer. "That's why Jack was mad. He thinks you're—"

"I'm not."

I turned in my seat to face him. "You swear, because I have hedge clippers and pitch forks and—"

He pulled off the road, taking an exit, which led to Rural King and Betty's Burgers and Baked Goods.

"Where are you going?"

"I have no idea. Someplace we can sit and talk."

The sign for Betty's, which depicted a grandma wearing an apron and holding a burger in one hand and a pie in the other, came into view.

"We can stop there." I pointed to the sign. We took a right and Grant pulled into the parking lot. The savory scent of burgers cooking on the outside grills drifted into the car.

"Whatever's going on between us is because we're attracted to each other, not because of some stupid contest."

Oh, how I wanted to believe him. Though the set of his mouth and the intensity of his fabulous blue eyes did make him seem sincere.

"Would you swear on a pair of hedge clippers that you aren't trying to make me the ringer?"

"I swear by all the sharp and pointy tools on your farm, I am not involved in that stupid contest."

He meant it, but that didn't change one horrific fact.

"Everyone thinks you are."

"Only the idiots." Reaching over, he grabbed my hand.

The warmth of his touch reassured me. Still, he wasn't the one people would be talking about. "In between classes, I heard some guys talking about a ringer. I didn't know what they meant at the time."

"It's not like I can idiot-proof the world, but at least you know the truth." His stomach growled and his gaze traveled to Betty's door. "Do the burgers taste as good as they smell?"

"Yes." What he didn't know wouldn't hurt him.

"Come on." He unbuckled his seat belt and opened his door.

Once we were seated in Betty's reading the menus, I gave him the good news. "Do you remember when I said Jack had to work?"

He closed the menu. "Please tell me your brother won't be touching my food."

"No. He works the cash register." I pointed across the room to the bakery display case where Jack stood glaring in our direction. I gave a small wave. He scowled and rang out the next person in line.

"And you didn't think to tell me this earlier...because?"

"You only asked about the burgers. Besides, I was hungry."

Muttering under his breath, he opened his menu. We placed our order and it wasn't long until I was biting into a burger hot from the grill.

"What's up with your friend's hair?" Grant asked.

There was only one person he could be talking about. "Delia is super-creative and she likes to be different. None of her clothes are the same as when she bought them. She colors on her jeans with markers, and cuts her shirts, and sews different pieces together. With the Wilton uniforms, all she can change is her hair."

"Aiden can't understand why anyone would color their hair pink."

"She's unique." Jumping to Delia's defense was my first instinct.

The tone of my voice must have clued Grant in. "He doesn't think it's a bad thing. Everything in his house is brown. He isn't used to color."

No surprise that serious boy came from a boring house.

"I couldn't live like that and I know Delia would go insane." We talked about our friends and school while we ate. Odd that it was comfortable, sitting with him like this. When the check came, he paid the waitress rather than going over to the cash register.

When we pulled up to the house, my grandma was crocheting on the porch swing. Crap. Goodbye any possibility of a goodnight kiss. As Grant's car pulled closer, she went inside. Thank you, Grandma.

He stopped in the drive and turned to me. "Are we okay?"

"There are no hedge clippers in your immediate future."

His eyebrows went up. "Immediate future?"

"Just leaving a little wiggle room in case you do something to tick me off."

He pointed at me. "Evil, scary girl."

"But not boring." I leaned in encouraging a kiss, and he met me half way. The happy sunshine feeling increased by about one hundred degrees and heat flowed through my body all the way down to my toes.

When he pulled away, there was an odd expression on his face. Was the kiss bad? Had I done something wrong?

Did I have bad breath?

"Zoe, I...never mind."

Was he serious? "No. It doesn't work that way. Finish what you started to say."

He leaned back against his door, so he wasn't touching me. Not a good sign. The heat I'd experienced moments before disappeared into a black hole of insecurity. "Spit it out."

"I like you. Tonight was fun. That's all I'm interested in. I'm not going to ask you to be my girlfriend."

Whack. His words hit me right in the gut. He didn't think I was good enough to be his girlfriend. Jack had been right all along.

Anger erupted inside of me and this time I let the lava spew forth. "Wow. You certainly think a lot of yourself. I wasn't expecting a ring and a promise of forever. I thought we'd date. Maybe it would turn into something more. Maybe it wouldn't, because sometimes you're a dick.

Thanks for the heads up that you aren't interested in anything serious, because I would've gone shopping for a wedding dress tomorrow." I shoved the door open, tossed my backpack onto the drive way and leveraged myself out of the car. It was like climbing out of a damn hole in the ground.

Slamming the door as hard as I could, I retrieved my backpack and stalked up to the house.

My grandma waited in the kitchen for me. When she saw my face, her smile wilted.

"What happened?"

I opened my mouth to speak and then checked the living room. "Is Jack here?"

My grandmother shook her head.

I told her about Jack's brotherly advice and how my evening had played out. "I'm just so mad because I thought Grant really liked me."

"Obviously, he's an idiot," my grandmother said.

"No argument there." I headed over to the kitchen cabinet where we kept the Tylenol, grabbed two, and poured myself a glass of water. "How I am going to get through Foods class? We have to work together."

"He'll be just as uncomfortable about it as you are. Boys tend to clam up when they're mad. Maybe he'll give you the silent treatment."

"If that's the best case scenario, I feel the flu coming on. You'll have to call me off school."

"Nope." My grandmother patted me on the back. "This is one of those suck it up and deal with it life moments."

I flailed in frustration. "I hate those moments."

"Sorry, unless you cover yourself in bubble wrap and live in a cave, they are unavoidable."

Chapter Five

Grant

Zoe took off like a rocket, shot up the steps to her front door, and went inside without looking back once. Why was she so mad? I was being honest. Wasn't that what girls wanted, a guy who was honest with them? I wasn't in the market for a girlfriend and I wasn't going to lie about it.

As I drove home, I could still smell the sweet scent I associated with her in my car. It smelled like vanilla. Maybe that was just because we were always baking. Who knew? Not that it mattered. There were plenty of girls out there who smelled good.

At school the next morning in the quad, I told Aiden about what had happened with Zoe.

"So things were going great, and then you screwed it up."

"That's one way to look at it." Not that I'd been looking at it like that.

"You swore off girls like Lena. Zoe is about the most opposite of Lena you can find."

He had a point. Before I could respond, someone tapped me on the shoulder to get my attention. Amber stood there, wearing the same pissed-off expression Lena used to wear when I'd done something that annoyed her.

"I heard the strangest rumor about you and that Zoe Cain girl."

"What did you hear?"

"Someone said you went to a hick bar with her last night."

"Not a bar, a restaurant." The hick part I couldn't exactly argue.

Amber crossed her arms over her chest. "I don't understand what you're doing with that girl."

"That makes two of you," Aiden said, like this was all very funny.

"Good to know you have my back." I clapped him on the shoulder.

Amber gave a dramatic sigh. "I don't know what you see in her—"

"It's none of your business who I see, Lena."

"Amber," she bit out.

41

Confused, I turned to Aiden. "Isn't that what I said?"

"No." He rocked forward on the balls of his feet. "You called her Lena. Probably because she's acting like a jealous girlfriend."

So that's why Amber looked like she wanted to stab me in the eye with a pencil. "He's right. I'm sorry, but I'm not in the market for a girlfriend."

"Your loss." Head held high, she stomped off.

"That was fun," Aiden said. "What are you going to do for an encore?"

"Shut up." I shoved him back a step.

He punched me on the shoulder, and we joined the other students heading to class. I couldn't help wondering if Aiden was right.

It's not like I could avoid Zoe, since we had Foods class together. How would she act when she saw me? Angry would be my first bet, and she would have access to knives, so I should probably try to smooth this over as much as possible. It wasn't even a date...we just stopped for dinner on the way home from detention. How mad could she be?

...

Zoe

In first hour class, Lena sat behind me, emitting rays of hatred from every pore of her body. Before the teacher came into the room, I gave her the good news.

"Grant's a dick. You can have him back."

She just blinked at me like she didn't know what to say. Students on either side of us stared at me, like I'd committed some form of sacrilege.

"But you were with him last night," Lena said.

"And that's when I realized he wasn't worth my time." I smiled at her and the students around me. "So anyone who was betting on me being the Ringer will have to put their money on someone else."

At lunch, Delia and I staked out the table we ate at yesterday and went to grab our food. I kept an eye out for Grant and Aiden. Not that they would be joining us. While we were in line, they came in and sat at a table across the room.

"Stop it," Delia said.

"Stop what?

"You watched until he walked into the room, and now you've glanced at his table twice."

Needing comfort food, I filled my plate with macaroni and cheese. Delia raised her eyebrows at my choice, but said nothing.

Once we were seated, she said, "Look on the bright side. Lena won't be gunning for you anymore."

"True, but how am I going to get through Foods class?" I'd enjoyed the proximity the tiny kitchen provided. Now I didn't want to talk to him, much less share a tiny workspace with him.

"Maybe Ms. Ida will let you trade partners."

"Doubtful."

"Whatever you do, don't let him know he upset you."

"I'm pretty sure he got the message last night that I was not a happy camper."

"Today, you need to pretend that you don't give a crap about him."

Right. Keeping my emotions in check wasn't one of my strong suits. I toyed with the mac 'n cheese on my plate.

"Eat." Delia moved my plate closer to me. "No guy is worth skipping a meal for."

...

Grant

At lunch, Amber tracked me down. She and her friend joined Aiden and me for lunch, which was a strange move, considering she'd wanted to kill me a few hours ago.

"Did you hear what Zoe told Lena in first hour?" Amber asked like she was thrilled with the news she was about to deliver.

"No." And I didn't care.

"Oh." Amber smiled at me and then poured dressing on her salad.

If she thought I was going to ask, she was wrong. And I doubted she'd sit on the information since she was obviously eager to share.

"I give it ten minutes," Aiden said, without looking up from the math assignment he was going over.

I checked the clock. "Five, max."

Amber talked with her friend, ignoring me. Exactly seven minutes later, she set her fork down. "I can't believe you don't want to know what she's telling the whole school."

Wait a minute. She's telling the whole school something? "Fine. What did she say?"

"She called you a dick and told everyone they'd have to bet on someone else being the Ringer because she didn't want a thing to do with you." Amber sat back, looking like she'd won some sort of bet. "Maybe you should stay away from hicks in the future." With that, she and her friend picked up their trays and moved to the table behind us.

Good riddance.

Aiden held his hand out. "Pay up."

I pulled a ten dollar bill from my wallet and handed it to him.

I couldn't believe Zoe was talking trash me. All I'd done was tell her the truth. I wasn't in the market for a girlfriend. "I bet I could get Zoe back, if I wanted to."

"You're on. But I wouldn't be so sure about that," Aiden said. "She doesn't seem like the forgive and forget type."

"I could do it."

"One question. Do you want her back or do you just want to prove that you can get her back."

"I'm not sure."

Aiden clapped me on the shoulder. "Like I said before, never a dull moment around you."

...

Zoe

When I stepped into the Foods classroom the first thing I saw was Grant talking to a pretty blond girl. Fabulous. Not only did I have to be near him every day, I had the added bonus of watching him flirt with other girls.

He chose that moment to make eye contact with me. I forced a look of disinterest and headed to my usual seat. What I needed was a distraction. Something else to think about besides the fact that I wasn't up to Grant's snobby standards. Maybe tonight I'd ask Grandma to take me out for some target practice with the shotguns.

Breathe, Zoe.

Calm thoughts.

Cool thoughts.

He was a jerk, and I was better off without him.

By the time Grant joined me at the table, my temper was manageable. Ms. Ida launched into a lecture about different types of icing we could make. To me, it was a no-brainer. The cupcakes were vanilla, so the frosting had to be chocolate.

Once we were back in our tiny claustrophobic kitchen, I gathered ingredients for chocolate icing.

"Aren't we going to talk about this?" Grant asked.

Had he realized he'd made a mistake last night? "Go ahead." I didn't want to start off in the wrong direction.

He pointed at the ingredients on the counter. "What kind of icing are we going to make?"

Pop. That was the sound of my bubble bursting. I opened a cabinet and pretended to search for something in case my expression gave my thoughts away. Since it was the spice cabinet, I pulled out a few more ingredients and set them on the counter. "I want chocolate."

He frowned. "I don't want chocolate. I want vanilla."

It was on the tip of my tongue to say, you can't always get what you want. Instead, I went with the less dramatic, "Fine. We'll make both."

He ran his finger down the list of ingredients for vanilla icing. "We don't have enough to make both."

Moving in close, I tapped the list. "Check out the recipe for chocolate icing. Notice anything?"

He scanned the recipe. "Like I said, we don't have enough for both."

How could he be so blind? "The recipes are the same except for the cocoa. All icing starts as vanilla before you add a different flavoring."

"They're all the same?"

"Pretty much." I unwrapped a stick of butter and put it in the mixing bowl.

Grant hovered over my shoulder, standing so close I could practically feel the heat coming off of his body. "Do you mind?" I asked.

"Do I mind what?"

Clueless male. I turned, put my hand on chest, and pushed him back a step. "I'd like a little personal space."

"Didn't seem to bother you last night."

He did not just throw that in my face. I gaped at him for a moment and then stomped down on my not appropriate language for school answer. "That was before I knew the real you."

"What does that mean?"

And I was done. Turning back to the mixer, I said, "We're supposed to be working."

He moved in close again so that his chest brushed my back. "We're supposed to be working together."

I clamped my lips together and stepped to the side, gesturing that he should take over. If he was operating the mixer he'd have to stay in one spot, and I could move away from him, which is exactly what I did.

Without adding the milk, he flipped on the mixer. *Poof.* We were enveloped in a cloud of powdered sugar.

I reached over and smacked the mixer off. Students laughed. Grant stood there looking surprised and confused. "What just happened?"

I coughed and waved the powdered sugar away from my face. "You should have added the milk first. And you never put a mixer on high when you're starting a batch of icing."

"Always read the recipe before you turn the mixer on." Ms. Ida's voice carried across the room.

"Now she tells me." Grant swatted at the fine layer of white dust coating the sleeves of his navy jacket, which didn't make much of an improvement.

I checked the mixing bowl. It was pretty much empty except for the butter. "Grab the powdered sugar from the cabinet and we'll start over."

He peered into the bowl. "A little bit of it's still in there. Won't that mess up the recipe?"

"We might need to add a little extra milk if it's too thick. Other than that it should be fine."

Working in silence, Grant added another cup of powdered sugar and the milk before turning the mixer on low. He paused like he expected another white cloud to attack him.

When nothing happened, he smiled at me.

It took effort not to smile back. Why did he have to look so good? "Go ahead and add the vanilla, and then take out half."

Once the icing was smooth Grant scooped out his portion and handed the bowl back to me. I mixed in the cocoa until the icing was glossy and brown.

Ten minutes later, we had successfully iced a dozen cupcakes. Ms. Ida circulated around the room, checking on everyone's progress. When she saw we'd made two flavors of icing, she beamed. "A bumpy start, but I knew you two would work well together."

I laughed.

"What?" Grant said. "She's right. We managed to work together and make something we both wanted."

"A bit ironic after last night. Don't you think?" I finished off my cupcake and grabbed another one.

He pointed at the cupcake I'd removed the wrapper from. "You're going to eat another one?"

"No one is guaranteed a tomorrow." Something my family was painfully aware of. "Life is short. Cake is good." It's not like I had to worry about being up to his standards.

"Time to clean up," Ms. Ida called out. "And I have an announcement. Wilton is hosting an auction which will include baked goods, to benefit the local library. If you're interested in participating, there will be a sign-up sheet by the principal's office."

Chapter Six

Zoe

Delia and I signed up to bake something for the auction. For one thing, it would take my mind off of Grant. For another thing, the students who raised the most money would be featured in an article in the school newspaper. Normally, I didn't seek the limelight, but after all this Ringer crap it would be nice to be known for something positive, which was why we were in my kitchen after school, flipping through my grandmother's cookbooks.

"We could probably find a cool recipe online," Delia said.

"According to my grandmother, that would be sacrilege. The recipes in these books have been handed down through generations of Cain women."

Delia pointed at the notes scribbled in the margins of a recipe for sugar cookies, which said, double vanilla. "It looks like they were altered by them, too."

"More vanilla makes everything better." I flipped through a few more pages. "What would be more impressive, a cake, a platter of cookies, or cupcakes?"

"We could make a cake surrounded by cupcakes and decorated with cookies," Delia said.

"Or," I said, "since the auction is Wilton raising money for a library we could make a cake shaped like a book."

"I like it," Delia said. "One question. Why do they host a fundraiser for the library, when half the families would probably donate the money outright?"

"I'm sure the answer is something like, 'Charity work builds character.'"

"Funny," Delia said. "I bet the people who need to build character won't be the ones participating."

Jack came in through the front door, bringing the smell of Betty's Burgers with him.

"Did you bring food home, or did you man the grills?" I was hoping for the first option.

He held up a family sized carry-out bag. "In honor of you realizing I was right about a certain snob, I brought home burgers and pie."

In his own obnoxious way, he was being supportive. "Thank you, I think."

He emptied the contents of the bag onto the counter. "Help yourself." Once he'd loaded up his plate he headed into the living room.

Delia and I put away the cookbooks and grabbed our own burgers.

"That was oddly civilized of Jack," Delia said.

"It's probably more about him being right than anything." I sighed in frustration. "I still don't understand why Grant had to be a jerk. He seemed so perfect."

"My mom says no guy is perfect, you just have to find one that makes you happy seventy percent of the time."

That was an odd equation. "What about the other thirty percent?"

"That's the time you fantasize about hitting him in the head with a frying pan."

I laughed. "So prince charming is a guy you only want to kill a third of the time? That doesn't sound right."

"No one's perfect." Delia squirted mustard on her burger. "So now that Grant and Aiden are out of the picture, who do you think is cute?"

Well, crap. "You don't have to stop liking Aiden."

"How could I like the best friend of the guy who was a jerk to you? That's against girl code."

"It's not like we need guys to have a good time. Let's go to the movies this weekend."

"Sounds good."

...

Delia and I drove into town to the multiplex. Everyone else seemed to have the same idea. The chick flick we wanted to see was sold out so we decided on an action movie. The usher led us into the theater. "There are only a few seats left together."

"The closer to the screen the better." If I came to the show I wanted the larger than life experience. Sitting way up at the back wall of the theater wasn't much different than watching television at home, and I could do that in my PJs.

We ended up a few rows from the front, on the aisle. I preferred being on the aisle so if I needed a refill on popcorn in the middle of the movie, I wouldn't have to squeeze past other people in their seats.

Delia pulled a bag of candy corn out of her purse and poured half of it into our container of popcorn. I took a bite of the sweet/salty mix and sighed in satisfaction.

"I can't believe you're eating that," a familiar male voice said.

"Aiden?" Delia turned around to see him sitting behind us. "Are you stalking us?"

"We were here first," Aiden said. The seat next to him was empty, but a black leather jacket was draped across the back of the seat. I couldn't tell if it belonged to a guy or a girl. Was Aiden here on a date or with Grant? I wasn't sure which would be more awkward.

"The usher led us to these seats." Delia pointed at the leather jacket. "Who are you here with?"

"Grant went to buy popcorn. Speaking of which, why did you put candy corn in yours?"

"It's good." Delia held our tub of popcorn out to him. "Try it."

"Not a chance," Aiden said.

The trailers came on blaringly loud, so Delia and I turned back around. What were the odds that we'd end up near Grant and Aiden at the show? It was like some higher power was messing with us. I kept my focus on the screen, even when I saw Grant coming back to his seat.

Once the movie started, I was swept away in the action. Delia and I managed to finish off the popcorn halfway through the film. Since the story was pretty brainless, I went for a refill.

Apparently, everyone else in the theater decided it would be a good idea to hit the concession stand at the same time. Every line was five people deep. No big deal. The plot of the movie wasn't hard to follow. The good guys were chasing the bad guys who'd committed fraud.

"It's busy tonight," the one voice I didn't want to hear said from behind me.

"It is a Friday." I was under no obligation to be nice to Grant since we weren't at school.

"True." He moved so he stood beside me. "What do you think of the movie so far?"

Should I move to another line to avoid conversation? No. I was here first. If he wanted to make small talk I could play along. "It's okay. We wanted to see Love Lost, but it was sold out."

"Really? Us, too." He said it so seriously, I almost believed him until he laughed.

"I'm sure it's better than what we're watching."

"There probably aren't even any fight scenes in that movie."

Had he not read the blurb? "I'm pretty sure the woman shoots the man because he cheated on her."

"And that's why it's called Love Lost—because she killed him?"

"I guess. I'm not sure how it ends." The line moved forward.

"Why would you want to see something like that?" He seemed to be genuinely asking rather than giving me crap, so I answered truthfully.

"Sometimes it's nice to get wrapped up in imaginary drama so you can avoid your own real life problems."

He shook his head. "I'd rather watch car chases and gun fights."

The line moved forward and our conversation was dead in the water. I avoided looking at him by reading the marquee style snack menu.

"Zoe, can we talk about what happened?"

Absolutely not. "Sure, why don't you call me later."

"We could talk now."

"Nope. I paid to watch the movie and that's what I plan to do." Luckily, the line moved forward and it was my turn. I asked for a refill on popcorn and then ran back to my seat in order to avoid any more awkward conversations with Grant.

The rest of the movie passed in a blur as my brain spun in circles trying to guess what Grant would've said to me. Not that it mattered. Unless he wanted to apologize, but even then, could I trust him?

I leaned over to Delia. "When the movie ends, we need to get out of here as fast as we can so I don't have to talk to Grant."

"Got it. If we hadn't paid so much to see this stupid movie, I'd suggest we leave now. I'm hoping the ending will be worth the wait."

Fifteen minutes later, the credits rolled.

"So not worth the wait." Delia stood and we made a beeline for the hallway, which exited back into the lobby. It was jam packed with people. We shuffled along with the crowd. By the time we made it out of the building, I was ready for fresh air.

"Where to now?" Delia asked as we crossed the parking lot to her truck.

I was stuffed full of popcorn and candy corn, so I didn't want any more food. "I'm not sure."

"How about The Art of Tea?" Delia loved the tea shop turned artist's studio where patrons were free to paint or draw on one of the group projects or create something of their own.

When we arrived at The Art of Tea, the parking lot was half full. Delia pulled into an open spot near the wide front steps which led up to the front porch where people sat drinking tea and working on looms.

"I don't understand weaving," Delia said. "Sewing is so much faster."

"I think it's supposed to be soothing, like meditation." I'd tried it, but had quickly become bored when I couldn't see any results. It takes a lot of threads to weave a blanket. I don't have that kind of patience.

We ordered raspberry tea and chose a table next to an easel with a half-finished painting. The canvas was covered in swirling lines of pink and purple. Delia sipped her tea and studied the picture. "This needs some more color."

She opened the baby food jars filled with paint and dipped her brush into the red. "Goodbye pink."

Delia would lose herself in the painting, which was fine by me. We came here to relax. I enjoyed the artsy vibe and I liked to people watch. My favorite people to observe were the ones who had no artistic talent but enjoyed the creative process anyway. They seemed so optimistic.

In the corner by the fireplace, I noticed something new. A sign read Crocheter's Corner. Intrigued, I went to investigate.

There were baskets of yarn, all leftover odds and ends which people probably donated once they'd finished a project. Coffee cups of crocheting hooks sat on an end table by the baskets. This was my type of art. I grabbed a ball of aqua blue yarn and a blue crocheting hook, because I liked to match the yarn to the hook, which I know is weird, but that's how my brain works.

I carried my find back to the table and made a single chain long enough to be a scarf. Then I double crocheted my way back up the chain.

Delia noticed my project. "We should tell your grandma that they've added yarn."

I doubted my grandmother would want to crochet with odds and ends. She read patterns and bought the exact number of skeins she would need and used the specific hook called for in the instructions. I preferred a more freeform approach, which was probably why she made beautiful afghans, which people paid good money for, and I had a collection of lumpy eclectic scarves that I gave away or donated to charity.

"She doesn't play well with others when it comes to sharing yarn." I'd learned as a young child that I was free to use any yarn in the open basket between the two recliners in our front room, but I wasn't allowed to touch any yarn in the picnic basket she used as a yarn caddy.

"True." Delia went back to painting, adding slashes of black while I lost myself in the repetitive motion of double crocheting.

...

Monday afternoon in the school cafeteria Delia and I tossed our backpacks on an open table and went up to make our trays. When we returned to our table Grant and Aiden were sitting there eating pizza like they had every right to join us.

I opened my mouth to ask Grant what he thought he was doing, but Delia breezed by me, pulled out her chair, and sat down like nothing was wrong. Since I had no idea how to handle the situation, I followed her lead.

Aiden held his hand out to Grant. "Pay up."

Grant pulled a ten dollar bill from his pocket and passed it to Aiden.

"What's that about?" I asked.

"I bet you'd go sit at another table before I had a chance to talk to you. Aiden said Delia wasn't the type to be chased off so easily."

"I'll take that as a compliment," Delia said.

"Wait. Should I be insulted?" I asked Delia.

"No. Your flare for drama is well known. Storming off would have been a good bet, but you probably would have yelled at him first."

Not like I could deny that. "Since we're being weirdly honest, Grant. What did you want to talk to me about? Keep in mind that I have access to sharp knives in Foods class."

"I am aware of that fact." He took a drink of his Coke. "Listen, I wanted to talk to you about what happened between us the other night."

"And you thought the crowded cafeteria would be a good place to do that?" I gestured at the room full of people.

"No. I thought maybe we could go grab coffee or a soda somewhere after school."

I teetered on the edge of a decision. If I went somewhere with him and we ended up fighting, I'd have to endure a very uncomfortable car ride home.

"Aiden, what are you doing after school?" I asked.

He blinked at me like I'd just confused the crap out of him. "Why do you ask?"

"Because if all four of us went somewhere, then Delia could take me home, thereby avoiding the quite possibly awkward car ride with Grant if what he says ticks me off."

"That makes sense," Delia chimed in. "So, Aiden, want to go grab a soda after school?"

"Okay." Aiden still looked like he wasn't quite sure what had just happened but decided to accept his fate.

Grant and I walked to Foods class together. Not like he was walking me to class, we were just walking in proximity. Once we were back in our kitchens mixing up a batch of cranberry orange muffins, I did my best not to ask him what he wanted to talk to me about.

"It's killing you, isn't it?" Grant ladled batter into the muffin tins with the ice cream scoop.

I pretended not to know what he was talking about.

"What?"

"You want to know what I have to say."

I rolled my eyes. "Right, because my world rotates around you."

I let my brother know that Delia was giving me a ride home, which was not a lie. I just didn't mention the part about spending time with Grant because I didn't want to listen to him gripe at me again.

Delia and I met Grant and Aiden at a coffee shop named Hallowed Grounds. Grant and I sat at a table in the back while Delia and Aiden sat at a table up front by the windows.

I stirred sugar into my café mocha and spoke in a quiet, calm tone. "So what's up?"

"The other night when I dropped you off, I was trying to be honest, and you freaked out on me."

"I did." And where was he going with this? I'd had every right to freak out.

"Why did me telling you I wasn't looking for a full-time girlfriend make you go ballistic?"

I stopped stirring and gaped at him. "That's not what you told me."

"Yes, it was."

"No. You said I was just someone to have fun with and you had no plans of asking me to be your girlfriend."

"Which is what I just said."

"No. It's not." How could he not see this? "You basically said I was the Ringer: someone you could have a good time with, but I wasn't real girlfriend material."

Grant squinted like he was trying to figure something out. "That may be what you heard, but that's not what I meant."

Hope bounced around in my chest. I did my best to flatten it. "Let's try this again. What exactly did you mean?"

"I have no plans to ask any female on the planet to be my girlfriend. I wasn't judging you or saying you were like the Ringer."

"Oh." That painted him in a much better light. "Well then I retract my freak out."

"You can do that?" he asked.

I nodded. "My world. My rules."

He shook his head. "You are a strange girl, Zoe Cain."

"But not boring." I took a big gulp of my café mocha and waited to see what would happen next.

"So is there anything else we should talk about?" He said this like he expected me to make some sort of confession. What was he getting at? And then I remembered. Crap. This was going to be awkward. I abandoned my drink in favor of turning my grandfather's watch around and around on my wrist. "When I was under the impression that you told me I wasn't up to your standards, I might have told Lena you were a dick, during first hour class...and other people heard me. I'd like to retract that, too."

He glared at me.

"Sorry." I stopped fiddling with my grandfather's watch, sipped my mocha, and waited to see how he'd respond to my apology. What I'd said hadn't been that bad. He couldn't be too mad, right?

The glare turned into a grin. "Actually." He slapped his hand down on the table. "I already heard about that."

"Lena told you?" Were they talking again? Had I inadvertently pushed him back into her arms? Cause that would totally suck.

"No. Amber."

Still sucked, but not quite as much. "Oh, I never would have guessed that one." I swirled my coffee around in my cup and waited. This moment, right here, was why I hated the whole dating system. I should be able to say, "So do you want to go out this weekend?" but if I asked him on a date I'd be labeled pushy. And I know Delia asked Aiden out earlier but that had sort of been a joke. So, I played with my drink, biding my time and waiting for him to make the first move.

He finished off his Coke and smacked the plastic glass down on the table. "Glad we straightened this out."

"Me, too."

He pushed away from the table, waved at Aiden, and then sauntered out of the coffee shop without looking back once. What the heck? That was so not how I hoped this encounter would end. Darn it.

Delia came to join me at my table while Aiden made his exit.

"What just happened?" she asked. "Aiden and I were talking and laughing and then Grant left and it was like Aiden had fulfilled some social obligation and he was done.

He just said, "See you tomorrow," and bailed on me."

"That's weird. It's not like they rode together."

"Makes me think they planned it this way." Delia frowned. "Maybe he didn't want me to accidentally think he was interested."

"That's crap. But, I'll one up you on weirdness." I explained my conversation with Grant and how we had straightened things out.

"So you apologized to him, and then he just left." Delia added creamer to her coffee. "At this point, I wonder if they're both just messing with our heads."

"Maybe. I do know one thing—your mom's frying pan theory is beginning to make a lot more sense."

Chapter Seven

Zoe

I gauged the emotional temperature of the room in first hour the next morning. Lena seemed content to ignore me, which was good news. I was afraid she'd hear that I'd been out with Grant. Not that we'd really gone out together, like a date, but someone could have seen us together in public and interpreted it that way.

As we walked down the hall after class, I asked Delia, "Want to practice making our book cake tonight?"

"Sure. I can give you a ride home. Do we need to stop at the store?"

"Have you met my grandmother?"

Delia laughed. "I know she's canned enough fruits and vegetables to last out the apocalypse, but I didn't know if she stocked up on flour and vanilla too."

"Fully stocked. The only thing we might want to buy is food coloring for the icing."

"I had an idea about that." Delia stopped walking and reached into her backpack. She pulled out a sketch of a book shaped cake, which used a Wilton green and blue striped necktie as a bookmark. "What do you think?"

"I like it."

She folded the paper and shoved it in her backpack.

"Cool. It's a plan. See you later."

"See you."

As I headed to Foods class, I wondered if Ms. Ida would have any ideas about how to make the cake stand out from the other entries. Maybe we could put gold on the edge of the pages like those classics books in the library. That might look good. I took a seat at my assigned table and opened my Foods book to the cake section where it listed different types of decorations. Sugar sprinkles for baked goods came in every color under the sun. Maybe we could use those.

"Earth to Zoe," a male voice said.

I blinked at Grant who was seated next to me at the table. "What? What'd I miss?"

"I said hello, but you were too busy staring at your book to respond."

"Sorry, I was trying to figure something out. Delia and I are working on ideas for the bake sale auction."

"So you're not just pining over me?"

"Nope." I shut my Foods book. "I hope that doesn't hurt your fragile ego."

He sighed dramatically. "Somehow, I will manage to survive."

Before I could respond, Ms. Ida clapped her hands to gain the class' attention. "Listen up, students. Today we are going to work on your cake decorating skills. I've placed a cake in each kitchen along with cake decorating supplies. Be sure to discuss with your partner what you'd like to do so that you are on the same page."

Curious, I headed back to our kitchen to see what we had to work with. Our cake was round. Our decorating supplies consisted of multi colored sprinkles, licorice, and a bowl of vanilla icing.

"What are we supposed to do with this?" Grant asked.

"Well it's round, so we could make a face or some sort of ball."

"Why would you want a cake that looks like a ball?"

"Have you never been to a little boy's birthday party where the cake was made to look like a soccer ball or a football?"

"No. The only cakes I've seen have had writing on them, as in 'Happy birthday to whoever.'"

"Once again, you've led a sad life."

"Once again, you're wrong. As long as the cake tastes good, who cares if it's decorated like a basketball?"

"Parties are about having fun. Decorated cakes are more fun than ones with roses." I picked up one of the Twizzlers and started peeling it apart. "We could make a baseball using these as the stitches."

Grant grabbed a Twizzler and followed my lead pulling the strands apart. "We could make a spider web cake."

"Or the licorice strings could be hair, like a Raggedy Ann doll."

Grant made a yuck face. "Who'd want to eat hair?"

"Hair is out, but you're good with eating a spider web?" I laughed.

"Spider man is always in good taste." He grabbed the bowl of frosting and stirred it with a spatula.

I grabbed another piece of licorice and tore it apart. "You have Spiderman pajamas at home, don't you?"

"Yes. Footy pajamas." He scooped up a dollop of icing and plopped it on the cake, then proceeded to smooth it out.

"Sexy." I laughed.

"Let me guess," he said. "You liked Disney princesses."

"Not that there is anything wrong with wanting to be a princess, but I was more of an Avengers Black Widow kick butt type of girl."

"Spiderman is way cooler than Iron Man and all his friends."

"Wrong." Once he'd finished icing the cake, I laid the licorice out in a spider web pattern. "How's that?"

"We need a spider man symbol or at least a spider." He left the kitchen and came back with a piece of plain white paper and a blue, black, and red ink pen. He sketched what appeared to be a fairly accurate spider man mask and then cut it out with the kitchen shears.

"Nice."

"Thanks, now how do we put it on the cake?"

"People put plastic things on cakes as decorations all the time. I think it's okay to put this on the cake. We could cover it with a thin layer of icing to make it blend in."

"Good idea." He used the spatula to smear icing on the front and back of the paper before pressing it into the center of the spider web.

Ms. Ida came around and nodded at our super hero cake. "Nicely done."

"Thanks." I smiled at Grant. "I guess we're not such a bad team, after all."

...

Grant

Zoe beamed at me, like everything was right in her world. And it might be, except for the fact that she was prone to drama and emotionally unstable. Even if I enjoyed spending time with her, she wasn't the type of girl I needed in my life. I needed someone low maintenance. Someone on the datable girl spectrum somewhere between Lena with her controlling ways and Zoe with her constant emotional upheaval.

I nodded like I'd heard what she said, but didn't really agree. "So, I guess it's time to clean the kitchen, again. That's the problem with cooking. You might end up with something good to eat, but the mess afterward doesn't seem worth it."

The happy expression slid from her face and she turned away from me. Walking over to the sink she filled it with hot water. "There's not much to clean today."

Her tone was flat, like she'd gotten the message I wasn't interested anymore, which was good. That would make everything easier. Aiden would see that I could have her back if I wanted her, so I'd win the bet, but I'd avoid the minefield of dating a girl who didn't really fit into my life.

...

My mother was absent from the dinner table that night. My dad sat reading something on his tablet.

"Where's Mom?" I asked.

"She had a meeting."

That cleared everything up. Still, this might give me the opportunity to get some answers to a few questions I'd been pondering. "How did you and Mom get together?"

He set the tablet down. "Why do you ask?"

"Well, I'm trying to figure out the kind of girl I want to date."

His gaze flicked to my mother's empty seat. "I'm not sure I can help you there. Your mother and I started dating my senior year at Wilton." He smiled like he was remembering something happy. "It was more her idea than mine. I was always lost in my books. More like your friend Aiden than you. Your outgoing personality definitely comes from your mother."

"So she just started following you around?"

"No, but she seemed to be wherever I went, and if she saw me she'd come sit with me and talk to me. At first, I thought she just wanted help with her homework."

I laughed. "So you were clueless."

He shrugged. "I never thought someone as beautiful as her would be interested in a guy like me."

"How'd you end up together?"

"One night, she told me she wanted to go see a play and asked if I'd take her. I said yes. After that I did whatever she suggested and everything seemed to fall into place."

What happened between my mom and dad being happy way back then and ignoring each other at dinner now? Could I ask him?

"I can see it on your face," my dad said. "You're wondering what went wrong."

"What happened?"

"Your mother chose me because I followed her lead and then she expected me to become someone I wasn't. I'm not the man who walks into a room and takes charge of a situation. I'm the guy who figures out the answers and happily turns them over to someone else to make the big announcement. I don't need outside validation. I'm content to think big thoughts and solve puzzles, and that doesn't give your mother the status she wanted."

And now I had no idea what to say. "Where does that leave you guys?"

"It leaves me eating dinner with my son while having an incredibly awkward conversation." He chuckled.

"And where does it leave Mom?"

"She finds her validation through charity work, and socializing, and you."

"Me?"

"Yes." He stared at me for a moment. "It's funny that you're turning out to be the sort of man she wished I was. We're both proud of you."

"Thanks." I ducked my head and concentrated on my food. "How about we end the awkward conversation portion of the evening and go finish our dinner on the couch while binge watching something on Netflix."

"Sounds good."

We adjourned to the den. I watched a series my father found on the SyFy channel while I contemplated my future. My mom was probably pushing me toward Lena because she'd recognized a kindred spirit but I did not want to go down that road. Where did that leave me?

...

The next day at school, I stood next to Aiden, scanning the crowd for a girl who would make my life easier, instead of causing more problems.

"She's over by the clock tower," Aiden said.

"Who?" I checked the area by the clock and spotted Zoe talking with Delia. "I wasn't looking for her."

"You're giving up?" He held out his hand. "Then pay up."

"Wrong. I could have her back in a heartbeat, so I win the bet."

"No way."

I filled him in on our conversation during Foods class.

"That doesn't prove anything. To win the bet she has to agree to go out with you."

"We never said that." Not that I couldn't get her to agree to go on a date with me. "Besides, if I asked her out, then she'd think I was interested and that's a problem I don't need."

"But you are interested." Aiden pushed his glasses up higher on his nose. "Or haven't you figured that out yet?"

"No. I'm not."

"Yes, you are. But that's okay because she likes you, too, and Delia is fun to talk to so it's a win-win."

"No. It's not."

"Is there another girl you're interested in?"

"I don't know. I haven't met all the new girls yet."

"I have. None of them confuse me like Delia. She's a puzzle I want to figure out."

And then my shy, sit back and let life happen to him friend headed straight for the one girl I didn't want to deal with.

...

Zoe

"Why does school have to start so early?" I finished off my coffee and stared into the bottom of my empty cup. "And how did my coffee disappear so fast?"

"I have a better and more relevant question," Delia said. "Why is Aiden headed straight for us with Grant."

I covered my yawn and glanced in the direction Delia indicated. My eyes were watering so I had to blink a couple of times before I could focus. I hadn't slept for crap last night due to some bizarre nightmares where I baked dozens of cupcakes, and Grant and Aiden bet on how bad each batch would turn out. And then Grant ate one from every batch, telling me they weren't good enough.

Delia was right. Aiden was headed for us like he had a plan and Grant was the one who appeared confused.

"What's that about?" I asked.

"We'll find out soon enough." Delia turned her back to the approaching boys and started talking about something she'd seen on television last night.

I nodded along like I was paying attention, because God forbid Grant think I was waiting for him to come bless me with his presence. He'd made it quite clear in Foods class yesterday that he did not think we made a good team. And at this point I couldn't agree more. I needed a guy who made me feel like I was important in his world, that I was more than good enough and he was grateful to have me around, not some moody snob who only wanted me on his terms.

"Good morning, Delia," Aiden said, walking around so he stood in front of her.

She backed a step away from him. "Morning. What's up?"

"Not much." Aiden reached out and touched the pink stripes of Delia's hair. "Why pink?"

"Technically, it's hot pink. And I think it's a happy color."

Grant sidled up so he stood next to me. Rather than talking, he nodded at me and said, "Hey."

"Hey, yourself." I yawned again. "Sorry, I didn't get much sleep last night."

"Stay up late binge watching something on Netflix?" he asked.

"No. I had bizarre dreams all night. When my alarm went off, it didn't feel like I'd slept at all."

Grant grabbed at my arm. "Where's your grandfather's watch?"

"Oh my God." I looked at my bare wrist. Cold panic shot through my veins. "It must have fallen off." I scanned the ground around my feet. Nothing.

"What's wrong?" Delia asked.

"My grandfather's watch. It's gone."

"It's probably in your car," Grant said.

"You guys look here. I'll check the car." My stomach twisted. I could not have lost my grandfather's watch. I dashed to the car and yanked open the passenger door. My heart beat faster as I scanned the seat, and the floor.

I heard footsteps running up behind. Had they found it?

"It's okay," Delia said. "I called your grandma. The watch is on your dresser."

"Thank God." I slammed the car door and leaned back against it.

We headed back to where the boys were still standing.

"Everything all right?" Grant asked.

I nodded. "It's always fun to start the day out with a panic attack."

"You must have been really tired this morning if you forgot to put the watch on."

I nodded. Since he'd inadvertently been the cause of my nightmares, I somehow felt this was his fault, which was ridiculous, but I wasn't feeling warm and fuzzy toward him at the moment.

The bell for classes rang.

Grant walked next to me as we headed into the building. "Do you have plans after school?"

"Yes. I plan on taking a nap." I yawned. Now that the high from the state of panic had worn off, I felt more tired than before. At this rate, I'd be lucky if I managed to stay awake through first hour.

At lunch, I sucked down a soda and prayed the caffeine gods would save the day. By Foods class, I wasn't doing too badly.

"You seem more alert," Grant said as we flipped through recipe cards Ms. Ida had passed out at the beginning of class.

"Caffeine is my friend." I stopped shuffling when I found a card for old fashioned mac 'n cheese. "We should make this. It doesn't require a lot of ingredients or a lot of clean up."

Our assignment was to pick a recipe and create a grocery list. We would only be allowed to use the items on our list when we cooked. So if we left anything off the list, we'd be screwed. Not that Ms. Ida had put it that way. Her message was more along the line of, you don't want to plan a meal and find out you don't have all the ingredients.

"Looks easy enough." He shot me a smile that had he not rebuffed me the day before, might have made my heart flutter. I wasn't about to go down that path again. Mr. Moody could find another girl to flirt with. Then again, what did I know? Maybe he acted this way with all females, whether he was interested in them or not.

"Why don't you write down the list of things we'll need," I suggested, "and then I'll double check it."

His smile faltered a bit.

I laughed. "What? Do you want me to write it down?"

"No. I've got this." He grabbed a pen and one of the blank recipe cards. When he was done, he passed me the list. I glanced at it. "You forgot butter and salt."

"We always have those things. Why would I need to put them on the list?"

"Weren't you listening? Ms. Ida said we could only use what we put on the list."

He snatched the card back and added the two missing ingredients.

"You don't like to be wrong," I teased.

"No one likes to be wrong. Not that I was. I just wasn't aware of all the rules."

I held my hand out for the card. "I better check again, just to be sure."

"No." He stood. "It's good. I'm going to turn it in."

"Whatever." Curious, I watched him approach Ms. Ida. As he made his way across the room, several girls glanced at him and smiled. He smiled back at every one of them. Was he preparing for a career as a politician, or was he just keeping all his options open?

...

Over the next few days, Aiden kept popping up near Delia. He wasn't flirting with her. It was more like he thought they were friends. More often than not, Grant came along for the ride. He flirted just enough to annoy me. Why was he flirting with me? Was he one of those guys that only went after girls who weren't interested in him?

Jack must have noticed what was going on, because Wednesday night at dinner he said, "I hear you're hanging around Grant again. What's up with that?"

Good question. I twisted my grandfather's watch around on my wrist. I'd been wondering that myself. "We have Foods class together, so we talk. It's not a big deal."

He tapped his fingers on the tabletop. "Does he come looking for you, or is it just in Foods class?"

"Some of both, I guess."

"You should know that guys are still saying he's trying to make you the Ringer, and he's not denying it."

Wait. What did that mean? "Did anyone ask him directly, or is he just ignoring stupid gossip?"

"You want me to ask him, because I'd be happy to do that."

That's all I needed. "Not a good idea."

"Tell me you aren't going to fall for this, Zoe. You're smarter than that, right?"

"I don't trust him. Does that make you happy?"

He nodded. "It's a start."

Delia was already in a conversation with Aiden when I approached her on the quad the next morning. Grant stood off to the side. When he saw me approaching, his face lit up, like he was happy to be in my presence. And I found myself smiling back. Maybe I should just come out and ask him what was going on. He probably thought we were just friends, like Aiden seemed to be with Delia.

I nodded at Grant. "Morning."

"Good morning." Pointing at my grandfather's watch, he said, "You must've gotten some sleep last night."

Okay. Small talk. I could do this. "I did, but I'm ready for the weekend."

"Big plans?" he asked.

"Yes. Naps interrupted by bouts of binge watching Netflix. There might be some cake baking in between."

He laughed. "Watch out, you'll end up on the evening news: Teenage girl goes on Netflix bender."

"That's a risk I'm willing to take." Bantering with Grant felt natural. We could be friends. Of course, it would be a lot easier to think friend thoughts if he wasn't so good-looking.

Chapter Eight

Grant

When I asked Zoe what she was doing this weekend, I thought she'd say, nothing, which was the standard girl response if she hoped you were about to ask her on a date. Not that I'd planned on asking her out, I was just filling the void left by my suddenly talkative best friend.

I had no idea what he was doing with Delia. Maybe he just wanted to be friends with her. Playing back-up to him was a strange new role, but it left me free to relax and talk to Zoe in a no-pressure situation, since I wasn't the one who initiated contact. Which made dating sound like interacting with an alien life-form. Where Zoe was concerned, that wasn't an inaccurate description.

She never reacted the way I expected, which was interesting. And she didn't try to tell me what to do or how to do something, which made hanging around her fun. It's like she didn't have an agenda.

Wait a minute...had I been friend-zoned? No way was I okay with that lame category. Maybe I should flirt with her just a little bit.

The bell for first hour rang, so we went our separate ways. Once we were out of the hearing range of the girls, I said, "What's going on between you and Delia?"

Aiden shrugged. "I don't know. I like talking to her."

"Are you going to ask her on a date?"

"I think we're good as friends, but I need to collect more data."

There was the Aiden I recognized. He didn't do anything spur of the moment. His entire life was planned out. "Ten bucks says you've created a spread sheet listing her positive and negative qualities."

"Of course I have, so no bet. At this point I don't have much information to go on. What about you and Zoe?"

"Nothing to talk about."

"Right. That's why you smile at her so much."

Did I smile too much? "It's called being smooth."

69

"I thought it was called keeping your options open, so you could win the bet."

"That too." What should my next move be? "Maybe we should see if they want to hang out this weekend. Not like a date, just something where we meet up with them."

"I'd be open to that, but you're in charge of making it happen. Talk to Zoe in Foods, see what you can work out."

I needed to mention something that the girls would want to attend no matter if we were going or not. I pulled out my cell and Googled local events. Apple butter festival, craft fair, outside screening of a movie I'd never heard of at a nearby park, and a pie eating contest at Betty's Burgers.

No, no, no, and hell no. I switched over to the new movies coming out this weekend. Thank goodness that Love Lost movie was gone. There were a few action movies which looked good, and a new Sci Fi movie about space vampires I wanted to see. Maybe I could steer Zoe toward that.

In Foods, I set my phone down on the table so Zoe could see what I was doing and pulled up the movie times.

"Anything good on?" Zoe leaned in so she could see the screen. The scent of oranges drifted up from her hair. What was that about?

"Oh." She pointed at the screen. "The space vampire movie is out."

Mission accomplished. "Aiden and I might go see it."

Zoe sat back and stared off into space. "I'll probably have to let Delia cut my hair to get her to see it with me."

"What's that mean?"

She laughed. "Delia prefers artsy films and I like paranormal and Sci Fi. In order to get her to go with me, sometimes it's necessary to bribe her by letting her mess with my hair or my clothes."

"Interesting. How does she get you to the Artsy movies?"

"I like to try new recipes, and she lets me use her as a guinea pig."

In a strange way that made sense. "Aiden will want to go. We could meet at the theater Saturday night and hang out afterward."

Zoe froze for a second, and then sat back in her seat and stared at me. "What does that mean? Hang out?"

Okay. Maybe this wouldn't be so easy. "I don't know. Just a no-pressure situation where we meet someplace and have fun."

"Like friends?" she asked.

I didn't want to label the situation, but I doubted Zoe would go unless I agreed. "Sure. That sounds good."

"So, if anyone asks you'll tell them we're just friends, right? Because I've heard that people are still talking about me like I'm the Ringer."

Now I understood where this was coming from. "If I hear any crap like that, I'll take care of it."

...

Zoe

"Are you sure this is a good idea?" Delia asked as we pulled into the parking lot at the movie theater Saturday night.

I pointed at my hair, which she'd foiled, adding cinnamon colored lowlights and cut to shoulder length last night. "Hello, you've already had your way with my hair, so there's no backing out now."

"Your hair looks awesome."

I flipped down the visor and checked out the new me. "It does, doesn't it?"

She nodded. "And I wasn't talking about the movie. I meant this whole hanging-out we're just friends agenda."

I'd been pondering Grant's reasons for suggesting this plan of action. "Maybe Aiden just needs a low pressure situation to feel confident, and if he has a good time then he'll ask you out."

"If I wanted to go out with him, why couldn't I ask him? Why do women have to wait for men to make the first move?"

"And so goes the dating lament females have been griping about since the beginning of time."

"You know Grant saying he just wants to be friends is a load of crap."

Maybe, maybe not. "Who cares? Space vampires and popcorn await us beyond those doors." I pointed to the theater and checked the time on the dash. "Let's go so we can grab good seats."

"What if the guys already have seats picked out?" Delia asked as we jogged across the parking lot to get out of the cool autumn air.

"If we don't like the seats we tell them they can sit with us in another spot. The joy of this not being a date is we don't have to worry about offending them."

"When have you ever worried about that?" Delia asked as she pulled the theater door open.

"It occasionally crosses my mind." I headed for the shortest ticket line.

After we purchased our tickets, popcorn, and soda we headed into theater four and scanned the dimly lit area for two familiar faces.

"They aren't here yet," Delia said.

"Then we can pick the seats." I headed toward the tenth row and sat in the second seat so Delia would end up in the third seat, allowing Aiden to sit in the fourth seat next to her.

"You should scoot over one more," Delia said, "in case Aiden and Grant want to sit next to each other."

"Nope." I took off my jacket and laid it on the chair next to me. "Grant can sit next to me, or he can sit on the floor."

"Okay." Delia placed her purse on the fourth seat and we waited. The lights dimmed, and the previews started.

Maybe they'd changed their mind. That would be a decidedly un-friendly thing to do. I checked the time on my cell. The movie was due to start in ten minutes. No need to panic yet.

"We don't need them here to enjoy the movie." Delia pulled a bag of candy corn from her purse and added it to the popcorn.

"You're right, but I'm going to be super-pissed if they bail on us since this was their idea. Bad things might happen to their cars."

"You better tell your grandmother to start a swear jar for bail money."

It was an old joke. Delia and I both had tempers which my grandmother was sure would eventually have her bailing us out of jail, at some point.

I picked at the popcorn and pretended to watch the previews. Where was Grant? If this had been some elaborate set up to mess with me, my grandmother really was going to need bail money. It was one thing to not be interested in me and suggest we hang out as friends. It was another superiorly shitty thing to invite me somewhere and then ditch me like it was some sort of stupid prank.

As the minutes ticked by, my mood nose dived. When the movie started, I sunk low in my seat ignoring the popcorn laced with candy corn Delia offered.

"Maybe they're just running late," she said.

"Doesn't matter," I lied. "We're here and we have popcorn."

At least the movie was interesting. I got sucked into the story and the ninety minutes flew by.

When the credits rolled, Delia glanced over at me.

"What did you think?"

"Considering the homicidal mood I'm in, it was pretty good."

Delia stood. "We're going to Art of Tea. I'll paint, you can crochet, and we'll plot different ways to vandalize Grant's car."

"Works for me."

We weaved through all the people in the lobby and headed into the parking lot toward my car.

"Hey, you're going in the wrong direction," Grant's voice called out.

Grant and Aiden came toward us smiling like everything was wonderful.

"No we're not." I crossed my arms over my chest and glared at Grant.

"What's going on?" Grant looked back and forth between me and Delia.

I forced a calm tone. "You asked us to come here and meet you to watch a movie together and then you didn't show up. That's what's going on."

Aiden reached up and rubbed the bridge of his nose. "Grant, did you and Zoe decide on the late show, or did you just assume she'd know that's what you meant?"

Grant moved a step closer to me. "You just finished watching the movie, didn't you?"

"And you thought we bailed on you," Aiden said.

I shrugged. "No big deal. It's not like this was a date."

"It's still a crappy thing to do but now that we've figured out what happened," Grant said, "do you want to go grab something to eat?"

"We were going to the Art of Tea, if you want to join us." No way was I changing my plans to fit what they wanted.

"Never heard of it," Grant said, "but I'm guessing they have tea."

"It's on old Main Street on the left hand side," Delia said. "It's a white two story house. You'll see people sitting on the wraparound porch working on looms."

"Looms?" Grant said like he hadn't heard correctly, or hoped he hadn't.

"Think of it as penance." I smiled sweetly at him and headed for my car.

On the drive across town, I said, "What's your spin on this?"

"Grant is an idiot."

I snorted. "Besides that."

"Sorry, that's all I've got."

Not like I could argue the point. The parking lot at Art of Tea was almost full. "I hope we can find a table inside."

"You go stake out a table and I'll grab two raspberry teas."

I spotted two open tables and chose the small round table by a window. It looked like an ice cream parlor table with just enough room to set drinks for a few people. A family of six came in and sat at the bigger table. I was glad I'd left the bigger table open. If I were to guess, I'd say the family was two kids with their parents and grandparents. My chest gave a familiar ache. I missed having my entire family together. No father and no grandfather left a big hole in my family gatherings. I was grateful for the people I had left. Even if Jack was obnoxious half the time.

Grant entered the establishment with a wary look on his face. Aiden scanned the area like he was analyzing the situation.

I waved when they glanced my way. Grant came toward me while Aiden headed toward the counter where Delia stood in line.

"What is this place?" Grant asked.

"It's fun." I pointed at the half finished paintings on the wall. "You can work on a community painting or start your own or try any other craft you want."

"What do you like to do?"

"I crochet." Standing up, I said, "Now that you're here I'm going to pick out some yarn. Be right back."

I browsed through the baskets of yarn and found a multi colored jewel toned skein of yarn which allowed me to choose one of several colors of crochet hooks. I went with emerald since it was larger than the others.

By the time I returned to the table, Delia and Aiden had joined us. Four mugs sat on the table. "Which one is mine?" I asked.

Grant pushed an elephant shaped mug toward me. "You are the proud owner of this hideously ugly mug."

"It is kind of bad, isn't it?" I laughed and picked the cup up by the trunk, blowing on my tea before taking a sip.

"I think Aiden wins second runner up for ugliest mug contest." Delia pointed at Aiden's mug which resembled a pumpkin missing its stem.

Grant held his black and brown speckled mug. "If I hadn't seen some of the other options, I'd think the lady behind the counter didn't like me."

Delia held up her delicate china cup covered in butterflies. "I must be her favorite."

Grant pointed at my head. "Cool hair."

"Thanks."

We made small talk and joked around for an hour, while Delia added circles and lines to someone's attempt at abstract art. "This person had no sense of balance."

"At least they tried," Aiden said.

"You should try it." Delia offered him the brush.

"No thanks." He pushed his chair back a little bit. "Not in my nature. Give me a page full of numbers and a problem to solve and I'm good. Don't ask me to paint or draw or God forbid, dance."

I leaned closer to Grant. "Want to learn how to crochet?"

"I'm pretty sure that's a skill I can live without."

"When the zombie apocalypse comes I'll have scarves and blankets. You'll be dependent on whatever is already in your house."

"That's a risk I'm willing to take."

"Are you sure?" I held out the six inches of multicolored scarf I'd crocheted so far. "I think you'd look lovely in a sweater made from this yarn."

"Nope. It's against guy code to wear that many colors at once."

I laughed. Hanging out with Grant like this was fun. He may not be boyfriend material, but he was entertaining.

When the conversation slowed, Delia stood and grabbed her painting. "I'm going to put this back on the wall for someone else to finish."

I looked at my off-kilter scarf.

"Shouldn't each row be the same width?" Grant asked.

"I prefer a free-form method. Besides, someone can unravel it and fix it if they want." After putting my project in the yarn area, and returning to the table, I said, "This was fun."

"Sorry about the time mix-up," Grant said.

"It all worked out in the end," I said. And it had, in a non-date way, which was the way it was supposed to work. "See you guys later." I headed for the door, leaving Delia to say her goodbyes. She joined me before my feet hit the bottom step of the front porch but waited until we were in my car to speak.

"That was fun in a weird platonic sort of way."

"Yeah, there was a definite lack of flirting this evening." It was like Grant had pitched camp on the other side of the dating line and he didn't want to cross it.

"I guess we'll just wait and see if anything interesting happens," Delia said.

Chapter Nine

Zoe

Monday morning I spotted Aiden and Delia drinking coffee together on the quad. Delia held two coffees, one of which should be for me, so she maintained her status as my best friend. Grant wasn't in the immediate area. Not that I was looking for him, but I thought it was a good idea to keep tabs on him to avoid any awkwardness.

Delia toasted my approach with one of the coffee cups and stepped away from Aiden. "Wait until you try this."

"As long as it's coffee, I'm good." I took a sip and tasted hot cocoa with a hint of coffee. "What is this?"

"It's the only way I drink coffee," Aiden said. "Half cocoa half coffee. That way it kills the coffee flavor."

"It's good." The downside to this concoction...did it only have half the caffeine? Because I was pretty sure I'd miss the normal amount.

The tone for first hour sounded. I shuffled along with the horde of half-awake students to first hour, congratulating myself on not asking Aiden where Grant might be.

Lena seemed half asleep during class, which was fine by me. Delia and I ate lunch together sans any males, friend or otherwise. And then it was off to Foods. Grant came to class late looking like he'd just rolled out of bed. I'd never seen him looking less than stellar, which made me think something had to be wrong.

Grant gave Ms. Ida a note and came to sit at our normal table.

"Are you all right?" I asked.

He nodded, but didn't say anything. I recognized his expression. It was the same one Jack had worn after my dad and grandfather passed away. His lips were tight and his eyes were narrowed.

I reached over and squeezed his forearm. "I know something is wrong. You don't have to share details, but I can listen if you need to talk."

He nodded, but didn't meet my gaze. Ms. Ida sent us back to our kitchens with instructions to measure out ingredients for mac 'n cheese. Not difficult. I filled the Ziploc bags and passed them off to Grant so he could write on them with a blue sharpie.

We were cleaning up when his cell beeped. He pulled it out and read a text. His response was immediate. He relaxed like a soldier who no longer had to stand at attention because the immediate threat had passed.

"Things are better now?" I asked.

"Yes."

"Good." Acting on impulse, I gave him a quick hug before heading off to grab my backpack.

...

Grant

I could breathe again. My dad had been taken to the hospital last night when he'd had a severe allergic reaction to some new food at a party. If my mom had been near him she would have told him he couldn't eat whatever it was, but she'd been across the room socializing and didn't realize what happened until after his eyes and throat started swelling shut. The EpiPen he'd had in his car had been out of date. An ambulance had been called. He'd been given steroids and was recovering in the hospital but my mother had sent me off to school because my pacing made her nervous.

The text from my mom said he was awake and apologizing for not being more careful. Maybe my mom's hands on approach wasn't such a bad idea. My dad was kind of like the absent minded professor type. He'd often become absorbed in his projects and forget to eat. My mom always made sure he was okay. Lately they'd been spending more time apart, which neither of them seemed to mind. Would this set them back on a path to being closer or happier? I hated that it took something like this, but I hoped it would help.

What Zoe had done, just being there for me without asking for anything was nice. I didn't have many people in my life like that who weren't family. And we'd had fun at that weird Art of Tea place. Maybe she was the type of girl I needed. Maybe I should ask her out, see if she wanted to try dating again.

I grabbed my backpack and jogged after her. She'd already gone into her classroom. I checked the time. We had a few minutes, so I waved at her from the doorway. She joined me in the hall. "Is everything all right?"

"It is. I just wanted to say thanks for being supportive."

"That's what friends are for." She smacked me on the shoulder. "You better get to class."

Friends. Oh, hell. I had been friend-zoned. I headed to my next class. I needed a plan. A plan to move me from the friend-zone category I seemed to be stuck in—for the first time ever. Not that I hadn't friend-zoned girls, but having it turned around sucked. I bet she was still interested.

"Everything all right?" Aiden asked when I sat behind him in class.

I nodded. "My dad's awake and talking."

"Good." He smacked me on the shoulder in the exact manner Zoe had. That settled it.

"I think it's time for me to get Zoe back."

Aiden's eyebrows came together like he was confused.

"For what?"

"Not like that. I mean I want to date her."

"Oh." He nodded. "That makes more sense. Think she's still interested?"

I glared at him. "Why wouldn't she be?"

He shrugged. "Seems like you two work as friends, like Delia and me. That's all I'm saying."

After class, I received another text telling me my dad was being released from the hospital. The rest of the school day flew by. Any problems paled in comparison to the worrying I'd done about my dad.

That night he slept through dinner, while my mother and I shared Chinese carry-out. Dark circles stood out under her eyes. "Are you okay?"

"I'm fine." She sipped her wine and stared off into space. "Actually that's a lie. I'm angry at your father for eating something he didn't recognize. He should know better than that. I'm angry at myself for not paying more attention to him."

I had no idea how to respond to that. "He made a mistake."

She set her wine glass down. "I've always taken care of your father. That was my role. Lately, I've backed off because he seemed to resent it."

"Dad told me that you guided him into asking you out." I chuckled. "He thought you wanted help with your homework."

She smiled, the first genuine smile I'd seen in awhile. "I kept waiting for him to take the lead. I grew tired of waiting and took control of the situation. Back then he didn't seem to mind."

Neither of my parents seemed happy with their marriage lately. Maybe my filter was off because I hadn't slept much last night because I said, "Are you guys getting divorced?"

"What? No. Why would you ask that?"

"It sounds like you used to be happy and now you're not."

"It's not as simple as being happy or unhappy. Everything isn't as black and white when you're a grown-up. You'll find that out one day. Speaking of which, I ran into Lena's mother at the party. She said you two aren't seeing each other anymore. Why is that?"

No way could I tell my mother that Lena's controlling ways, which seemed to be the same way my mother treated my father, made me feel trapped and claustrophobic. "We wanted different things."

"Are you seeing someone else?"

"I've gone on a few dates. Nothing serious."

"A girl like Lena would be an asset to your life. Remember that. There will be a window of time where you can get her back. If you wait too long it will be over."

Later that night, my dad felt well enough to sit in the living room. His eyes were bloodshot, and he looked older than he had the day before.

He caught me studying him. "Go ahead and say it."

"Say what?"

"I'm sure your mother told you about how I let the EpiPen in my car expire and how I should have known better than to try something without first asking if it was nut free."

"You made a mistake. No big deal." I tried to sound like I meant it, but wasn't sure if I succeeded. "Mom's not blaming you."

"Right." He settled back into his chair. "Assigning blame is one of her specialties."

Now my dad sounded like a jerk. I didn't know how to respond, so I turned the volume up on the television. Maybe zombie aliens would improve my mood.

...

Zoe

Delia and I practiced our cake baking skills Wednesday night after school. Our book cake came out a little lopsided. "What's that supposed to be?" Jack asked.

"It's supposed to be an open book." We'd made a nine by thirteen rectangular cake and then added two square cakes on top to represent the pages.

"Looks like a Lego," my brother offered.

He wasn't wrong. "I think we need to see if we can find any cake pans shaped like books."

"In the meantime," Delia grabbed the bowl of frosting off the counter and dropped a glop of it onto the cake, "we can ice this and eat it while we cruise Google for a cake shaped pan."

Jack grabbed a hunk of cake and took a bite. "It might look weird, but it tastes good."

"Thanks." I took a bite and realized he was right. "Maybe we need another plan for the fundraiser. I don't want to spend money on a pan."

"Maybe we just make it a closed book and use the rectangular pan. That would be easier." Delia shoved a spoonful of icing in her mouth.

I doubted a plain rectangular cake would bring the highest donation. "I want something with more flair."

Jack cut another hunk of cake. "You keep working on it, and I'll help get rid of the rejects."

"Gee thanks," Delia said.

"Happy to help." Jack wolfed down his cake and exited the kitchen leaving his dirty plate on the counter.

I would have yelled at him, but I was grateful he was relocating so Delia and I could talk.

"Is it me," I asked, "or does it seem like Grant is flirting with me?" He'd been oddly attentive before school and he'd sat with us several days at lunch.

"It's not just you. He seems to be making a move again. Maybe he figures if Aiden ever asks me out then he should ask you out."

"That's flattering. Dating by convenience."

Delia laughed. "Hey, if you like him, does it matter why he asks you out?"

"Yes." I put the dirty dishes into the sink and rinsed them off. "I want someone to choose me because he likes me. Not just because I'm there. This conversation is stupid. It's not like he's asked me out. He could just be flirting because that's how he treats all girls."

"He doesn't flirt with Amber." Delia opened the dishwasher and frowned when she saw they were clean. "Crap. Do you want to empty the clean dishes or do the dirty dishes by hand?"

"Hand me the silverware basket." I took the silverware from Delia and put it away while she put the glasses in the cabinet above the sink. "If Grant is flirting, what's his agenda?"

"I have no idea."

"I'm guessing he'll want to date, but not exclusively." I finished the silverware and grabbed a stack of plates. "Is it wrong that I don't want to just date?"

"Maybe that's how all couples start out because guys are afraid to commit," Delia suggested.

Was she right? "Once again, this is a stupid conversation because he hasn't asked me out. Why am I worrying about something that might not even happen?"

"We're teenagers. Isn't that what we're supposed to do?" Delia asked. "Be all angsty about our lives?"

I laughed. "True. Instead of being angsty let's make plans for the weekend."

Delia put away the last clean dish. "I did your hair last weekend, so that's out."

The phone rang. Caller ID showed it was my cousin Jane. "Hello, cuz. Long time no see."

"That's exactly why I'm calling. Want a visitor, or maybe two, this weekend?"

"You're in luck. Delia and I were just discussing our lack of plans."

"Problem solved. You'll hang out with your fabulous cousin and her new boyfriend."

"Oh, okay." My enthusiasm dwindled. Not that I wasn't happy for Jane, but being a third wheel was never a good idea.

"Stop that," she said. "No one will be a third wheel."

"When did you become psychic?" I asked.

Jane laughed. "I know you. Don't worry. Nathan's dad arranged for him to spend time in a lab job shadowing people doing scienc-y things."

"Scienc-y things?" Jane always had a way with words.

"It's a technical term. Anyway, Nathan will do his thing while I spend time with you. Then all of us can go to a late lunch together. Delia is invited, of course."

"Hold on." I moved the phone away from my mouth and explained the plan to Delia. "Sound good?"

"Can I mess with her hair?" Delia asked.

I laughed. Delia had been trying to get her hands on Jane's hair for ages. Not that there was anything wrong with it, but Delia claimed that Jane wasn't using her thick straight hair to its full potential.

"Absolutely not," came through the phone loud enough for both of us to hear.

...

Jane arrived on my front porch wearing what looked like pirate boots, skinny jeans, and the fuzziest sweater I'd ever seen. When I hugged her it felt like I was grabbing a bunny.

"What's with all the fluffiness?" I asked.

She rolled her eyes. "Nathan gave me this sweater. I figured if I wore it here the only people who'd see me would be you two and some strangers."

"So he's not the perfect guy?"

Jane pulled her cell from her bag and pulled up a picture. She passed the phone to me. A dark haired guy with dark eyes and a jaw like one of those Greek statues smiled at me. "Wait. I changed my mind. He is perfect."

Jane snatched her phone back. "He's a hottie, but his taste in clothes is suspect. I Googled the designer name on the label, and this ridiculous sweater cost more than my entire wardrobe put together."

I led Jane into the living room where we sat on the couch. "Is that because you treasure hunt for your clothes at Goodwill, or do you mean normal clothes?"

"Regular clothes." Jane held out her arm and blew on the inch long strands of turquoise fluff, which seemed to grow from the fabric. "He said his mom helped pick it out."

"It's a pretty color," I offered.

Someone knocked on the front door, and then opened it. Delia bounded into the room and started to say hello, but then she laughed. "What is that crime against fashion you're wearing?"

"A gift from a wonderful guy whose mother might hate me," Jane said.

Delia tilted her head. "Maybe she thinks you're precious and wants to wrap you up in soft fuzziness, so you won't get hurt."

"Right. This sweater leads me toward our mission for today. It's called Operation buy me a new shirt. I'm going to spill a soda on this one as soon as we get to the mall. That way I don't have to wear it all day."

"Nice solution." I stood. "If we leave now we'll be at the mall when the doors open."

Jane checked her cell for the time. "Have I mentioned that if you moved to Greenbrier there would be a mall fifteen minutes from town?"

"You can order anything you want from Amazon," Delia said. "I've seen Greenbrier. There aren't enough houses with wraparound porches."

"And you live on top of each other," I added. After growing up on a farm with acres of land, Jane's house seemed like it was surrounded on all sides, plus the backyard was the size of a postage stamp.

"It's called suburbia," Jane said. "It comes in handy when you want a pizza delivered."

"I parked behind Jane in the driveway." Delia shot me a conspiratorial look. "Why don't I drive?"

"We won't fit in your truck," Jane objected.

"My car is on the side of the house." I changed directions and headed for the side door. Delia and I had planned this out in advance because even though I love my cousin, she's not the best driver. She seemed to think turn signals were optional. After one too many heart pounding experiences as a passenger in her car, both Delia and I plotted to avoid her driving us.

The trip to the mall took forty-five minutes, during which time Jane told us stories about Nathan and we filled her in on our not quite love lives with Grant and Aiden.

"Maybe you should make Grant cupcakes," Jane suggested.

"Why would I do that?"

"It worked with Nathan," Jane explained how she had baked cupcakes for lunch every day.

"It's like the Betty Crocker method of dating," Delia commented. "Do you still make him cupcakes now that you're his girlfriend?"

"Yes," Jane said, "because I love to bake."

"That must run in the family," I said as we parked at the mall. "Now what's our first stop?"

"We need to go to the food court so I can spill a drink on my sweater," Jane said. "One of you will have to bump into me, on accident, of course."

"You couldn't just spill it on yourself, on purpose?" Delia asked. "And then tell Nathan that we bumped into you?"

"I would never lie to my boyfriend." Jane seemed offended by the suggestion.

"But you won't tell him that you don't like the sweater." I held the door open. As we entered the mall, Muzak assaulted our ears.

"In theory, I love this sweater because it was a gift from him," Jane said. "I just don't necessarily love the design of the sweater."

"Glue some eyes on that thing and you could be a Muppet," I teased.

After taking care of Jane's sweater situation, we hunted through sales racks of shoes. I spotted a pair of turquoise boots and pointed them out to Jane. "Those would match your fuzzy beast of a sweater."

Jane touched the suede boots like she was petting them. "These would almost make wearing the sweater worth it."

I picked up a pair of navy high tops. "Think I could wear these with my school uniform?"

"You could," Delia said. "They'd make you change as soon as they noticed, but you could wear them."

"A school dress code." Jane shuddered. "I can't imagine."

"The real pizza in the cafeteria makes up for it," Delia said.

"I thought it was the handsome male students," a familiar masculine voice said from behind me.

I laughed and turned to see Grant standing in the men's shoe section across the aisle. "You're right. How could I possibly forget that?"

He closed the distance between us, pointing at the high tops I held. "Aren't those a little small for your brother?"

"They're girl's shoes." I held them up, showing him the box even though I knew he was teasing.

"No." He shook his head. "They're not."

"Who's the shoe critic?" Jane asked.

"Grant this is my cousin, Jane."

He nodded at her. "Nice to meet you."

"You, too," Jane said.

Delia not so subtly glanced around. "Where's your partner-in-crime?"

"Aiden hates the mall. Too many people."

"Not the extroverted type, huh?" Jane asked.

"No." Grant's phone buzzed. He checked the screen. "I have to go. See you at school."

"See ya." I watched him walk away. Once he was out of sight, I turned to Jane. "Thoughts?"

"He took the time to tease you about the shoes, so he put effort into speaking to you which probably means he likes you," Jane said.

"Maybe." I put the shoebox down. "Let's go look at purses."

We spent another hour wandering the mall until Nathan texted Jane. She frowned and texted back.

"What's wrong?" I asked.

"He wants me to meet him and some other people for lunch rather than him eating with the three of us."

Delia crossed her arms over her chest. "That's rude."

"Agreed." Jane tapped away on her cell. "I'm telling him that we already made plans to go out to eat together and he's welcome to join us."

"Are you sure you want to do that?" It seemed like a bold move.

Jane nodded. "I really like Nathan, but sometimes he acts like the world rotates around him."

"Aren't all guys like that?" My brother expected everyone to do what he wanted. My dad had ignored my mother when she told him not to drive a classic muscle car that didn't have air bags. He'd laughed at her concerns. A few months after that argument, he was dead. Tears filled my eyes. Would this ever stop happening? Being ambushed by grief had become a regular event over the last year. The frequency had lessened. The emotional wound wasn't raw anymore, but it still hurt.

"You okay?" Delia asked.

"Give me a minute." I closed my eyes and took a few deep breaths, focusing on the moment. Thinking about how my dad would want me to be happy. Once I felt in control I opened my eyes. "Sorry. That one snuck up on me."

"I think it's time for coffee," Delia said. "That always makes you feel better."

Jane rejoined us with a smile on her face. "Nathan will meet us for dessert. All I have to do is text him with the name of the restaurant when we're almost done eating."

"Sounds good. Right now I need a café mocha." I pointed toward the mall. "Starbucks is this way."

"Where are we going for lunch?" Delia asked.

"That is a question we can discuss over coffee."

Once we were seated with our caffeinated beverages, Jane asked, "What restaurant has the best desserts?"

"Betty's has the best pie," Delia said.

Jane frowned. "I'm not a pie person. I don't understand why people make such a fuss over warm fruit."

"Because it's awesome," Delia said. "But if you want cake we can go to Frank's BBQ."

"Why are all the restaurants around here named after someone?" Jane asked.

"Because they aren't chains," I said. "They are family owned and operated, which makes them better."

Jane pointed at my mocha. "How's that chain coffee tasting?"

"Starbucks is awesome but they are the exception to the rule."

After some more shopping we headed to Frank's as planned. I was halfway through my plate of barbecued ribs when Jane texted Nathan.

"I want to be sure and give him enough time to meet us."

I hoped Nathan was as wonderful as she thought. In my limited experience, most boys didn't live up to the way guys were portrayed in movies. When Nathan entered the restaurant half an hour later, I realized he could definitely play a leading man. Jane's face lit up when she saw him and I was relieved to see him beaming right back at her. Of course that didn't stop half the women in the restaurant from checking him out. Not that I could blame them. If he wasn't dating my cousin I'd be staring at him, too.

He arrived at our table, sat down, and kissed Jane on the cheek. "Hello."

She blushed. "Hello, yourself. Nathan, meet Zoe and Delia."

We did the normal nice to meet you round of introductions, and then Nathan tilted his head and touched the sleeve of her turquoise yet far less fuzzy replacement sweater. "What happened?"

Jane ducked her head. "I spilled a drink on my sweater. Sorry."

He stared at her for long enough that the situation became uncomfortable. "You don't like the sweater."

"Of course I do." Jane sounded slightly panicked.

"Let me rephrase that. You don't have to like the sweater just because I gave it to you."

"I do. End of discussion." She snagged the dessert menu from the center of the table. "More importantly, do you want to split the carrot cake and the crème torte or should we switch one of those out for German chocolate cake?"

"The first two sound good," Nathan said.

"Vegetables don't belong in cake," Delia muttered as she looked at the dessert menu.

"Most don't," I agreed. "Carrot cake is a wonderful aberration."

We made easy small talk with Nathan while we ordered and then ate dessert. I could see why Jane liked him. He said all the right things and told funny stories but he reminded me of someone running for political office. He was a little too smooth and perfect to be real. Then again, who was I to judge? I'd just met him.

Chapter Ten

Grant

I heard voices coming from the dining room as I headed out the door, Sunday morning. One of them sounded disturbingly familiar. I froze halfway down the hall.

My mother stepped into the hallway and smiled like everything was right in her world, which confirmed my suspicion. "There you are. Come join us. Lena and her mother dropped by with scones and coffee."

I pulled my keys from my pocket. "Sorry. Aiden is waiting for me."

"Then come say hello before you leave."

I could make a break for it and run out the door, but the grief I would receive over my rude behavior wasn't worth it. "Of course."

I stepped into the dining room, ready to nod, say hello, and run like hell, but I didn't manage to get a word out. For a moment, all I could do was stare, and I knew I was being an idiot, but my brain was having trouble processing this unexpected development. Lena, my controlling and manipulative ex-girlfriend had transformed herself. Gone was her standard ponytail. Her hair was cut short in a way that made her eyes look huge and her bright red lips kissable. "Your hair." Was all I managed to get out.

"Do you like it?" she asked, like she wasn't quite sure it had been the right move.

I nodded, afraid of what might come out of my mouth.

"Thank you. I was in the mood for a change." She pointed at the platter of pastries on the table. "You should try the cranberry scones. They're amazing."

"Sure." I sat down and picked up a scone, even though the rational part of my brain was screaming at me that this was a trap. If I sat here and made small talk, I'd end up agreeing to do something else with Lena.

My mother and Lena's mom had their heads together while they pored over some decorating magazines. "What's that about?" I asked, trying to take control of the conversation, at least.

89

"Mother wants to redo the screened in porch and turn it into one of those all season rooms with glass walls and a fireplace."

I took a bite of the scone, not tasting it. Lena was smiling at me and my mother was smiling at me and I needed out of this room before the two of them somehow managed to screw up my life. Pushing away from the table, I stood. "Nice seeing you. I have to go. I'm meeting Aiden."

"Where are you meeting him?" my mother asked.

Wherever I said I was going, my mother would suggest I take Lena along for the ride. Come on brain. Think. Where would Lena not want to go?

My cell buzzed. Talk about divine intervention. "Excuse me." Aiden's name flashed on the screen along with a text that he needed more sleep so he didn't want to do anything until later.

"Something wrong?" Lena asked.

I knew she could see the screen and the message from where she sat, which meant I was doomed, unless I acted fast. "I should call him."

Lena leaned in close and whispered, "You're terrified your mother will suggest you and I do something together, aren't you?"

She didn't sound mad, like I thought she would. "Maybe."

"Don't worry. I see now I may have been a little pushy before. I'm trying not to be that person anymore."

What did I say to that? "Oh...that's good."

My mother asked Lena a question about the all season's room, passing her a magazine. I ate my scone while I calculated my odds of escaping the dining room without my mother manipulating me into doing what she wanted.

Lena passed me the magazine and pointed at two photos.

"Which one do you like better?"

"They're both nice."

My mother laughed. "That's exactly what your father would say if I asked him, which is why men are no help when it comes to decorating."

And here was my opening. "Since I can't help, I'm going to take off now. It was nice seeing both of you." I nodded at Lena and her mother as I beat a hasty retreat to the garage, my car, and freedom. I didn't have a destination. I just wanted to drive so I headed for the highway.

That hadn't been so bad, after all. Lena wasn't acting at all like her old self. Had she changed? She'd always been beautiful, but her new hair made her hot. It was just hair. Still. She'd looked amazing.

The buzz of the pavement under my tires had my mind wandering to the good times Lena and I used to have together. Wait. Why was I doing this? Did I want to get back together with her? That was ridiculous. What were my other options? Amber had become annoying. Zoe's face popped into my head. Maybe I should talk to her. See how I felt when she smiled at me.

Consciously or not, I found myself driving toward the exit for Betty's Burgers and Zoe's house. I pulled into the parking lot at Betty's. I needed to think this through before I did something stupid. If I'd learned anything from my relationship with Lena it was that breaking up with someone was no guarantee they'd be out of your life. Unless one of you moved to another city, you still had to see the person at school and around town. Did I really want to start something with Zoe when I'd have to see her every day in Foods class?

A knock on the window brought me out of my thoughts. Zoe stood there smiling. Delia was on her cell. I rolled down the window. "Hello."

"What are you doing here?" Zoe asked as she leaned down to talk to me.

"Learning how to play violin, obviously."

She rolled her eyes. "Let me rephrase that. What are you doing in my neck of the woods?"

"Hiding from my mother." Wait. Why did I say that?

"I see." Zoe tilted her head to the side. "So, this is like witness relocation for snobs?"

"Exactly. What are doing today?"

"Delia and I just finished eating. We were thinking about playing putt-putt golf since it's so nice outside. Want to join us?"

It's not like I had any other plans. "Sure. I could call Aiden and we could meet you guys."

"Sounds good."

I dialed Aiden's number and explained the situation.

"I'm sleeping," was his answer.

"Throw on some clothes and meet us at Putt-Putt Village." I hung up, not giving him a chance to back out. "Aiden's in. He'll meet us there."

On the twenty-minute drive to my destination, I ran through a dozen different scenarios of how dating Zoe could turn out. None of which helped me figure out what I wanted to do.

I met up with Zoe and Delia in the parking lot. We sat on a park bench while we waited for Aiden. Zoe told me about her cousin and the guy she dated.

"Why would she tell him she liked the sweater if she didn't? Guys don't want to be lied to."

"If you gave a girl something and she told you to return it, how would you feel?" Zoe asked.

"I wouldn't be happy, but it's better than finding out later that she lied."

"So honesty is always the best policy?" Delia asked.

There was a note of challenge in her voice.

"Yes," I said and then looked at Zoe.

She tapped her nails on the bench. "I'd say almost always, unless you're bending the truth to save someone's feelings."

Once Aiden joined us, we each paid for our own golf balls and grabbed a putter. Zoe went first, smacking the ball too hard so it rebounded off several obstacles and rolled back to the starting line.

"You do realize that the point of this game is to make your ball go in the other direction, don't you?" I pointed toward the hole.

"Smart ass."

I laughed. "Let me show you how it's done."

I tapped my ball and it rolled through the obstacles and stopped a foot from the hole.

"That's a boring way to play," Zoe said.

Delia hit her ball so it ricocheted off several obstacles, and made a hole in one.

"That shouldn't have happened," said Aiden.

"Why not?" Delia asked.

"The angles don't work that way. If you look at it mathematically, you should've ricocheted the ball off the second obstacle to make a hole in one."

Delia shook her head. "It's not about math. It's about balance and patterns."

"We'll see." Aiden lined his ball up, tapped it and sent it smacking into the second obstacle and into the hole. "That's how it's supposed to work."

"You play your way, and I'll play mine."

By the last hole, Delia and Aiden were tied for first place. I was in second and Zoe was in a distant third.

"Maybe if you aimed the ball, it would work better." Delia said to Zoe.

"That would be boring." She whacked the ball and ended up bouncing it off the green onto the sidewalk. Rather than being upset, she picked up her ball and waited for us to finish.

"Good thing we aren't playing for money," I said.

"We're playing for fun," Zoe said. "My way is fun for me."

"Even though you won't win?" Aiden asked.

"I don't really care about winning this game," Zoe said.

"Don't let her fool you. There are games she's prepared to spill blood over." Delia lined up her shot, and ricocheted the ball off the wall three times before it dropped into the hole.

Aiden made a pained sound. "How are you defying the laws of physics?"

"It's making you crazy, isn't it?" Delia sounded like she was enjoying the situation.

"Yes," Aiden said. "You're systematically destroying the rules of my world. Knock it off."

"Change is good for you." Delia gave an evil laugh.

"No. It's not." Aiden lined up the angle of his putt, and then tapped the ball a little too lightly. It headed straight for the cup but stopped an inch from the hole.

"Woo hoo!" Delia threw her arms up. "I win."

Aiden muttered under his breath as he knocked his ball in, adding an extra stroke to his score. I hit my ball in after three tries.

...

Zoe

While I watched Delia run a victory lap around Aiden, Grant grabbed my hand. What was that about?

"Come here a minute." He tugged me toward the counter where we returned our golf clubs and then over to one of the benches lining the sidewalks.

Holding his hand felt frighteningly natural. My stomach knotted up. What the heck was Mr. I-don't-want-a-girlfriend doing?

He looked at our entwined hands as he spoke. "I like you, Zoe. And not just as a friend."

And now it felt like I had swallowed a dozen golf balls. I waited for him to continue, hoping my palm wouldn't start to sweat.

"Do you want to try dating again?" He glanced up at me with a strangely vulnerable look in his eyes.

Yes, my inner girly-girl squealed. I stomped down on her enthusiasm, forcing myself to be rational. I'd been down this path before and been deeply disappointed. I needed more information this time around. "When you say, dating, what does that mean?"

He shrugged like it was no big deal. "It means we spend time together, and see what happens. No promises of forever, but with the idea that it could turn into a boyfriend girlfriend thing if it works out."

That sounded pretty good, but I needed more...some sort of guarantee that he'd be sticking around for a while.

"I'll agree on one condition."

"What?"

"There's a dance coming up at school. Will you take me?" I needed to know that my brother had been wrong. Grant needed to prove that he thought I was good enough to take to a big event.

His eyebrows came together like he was figuring out all the ways this could go wrong, which was weird since he was the one who'd started this. Time to smooth things over so he'd know I wasn't trying to trap him. "This is not me trying to be your exclusive girlfriend. This is me wanting to disprove my brother."

"What do you mean?"

I told him about my brother's opinion that snobs never took hicks to big events.

"Your brother is an ass."

"Some days yes, some days no. Here's what I'm suggesting: we date like you said and see where it goes. As long as we're still dating when the dance happens, we go together."

"I can live with that." His cell vibrated, like he'd received a text. He dropped my hand to grab his phone. His eyebrows went up and then he laughed. "My dad says I need to come rescue him because my mother and Lena's mom have him cornered in the dining room and they're forcing him to look at decorating magazines."

That was strange. "Why is Lena's mom at your house?"

"Probably because her dad didn't want to talk about wallpaper and carpet, either." He stood. "I better go save him."

"How will you do that?"

"He just bought the collector's edition of Doctor Who. We're up to the sixth season. If I suggest they watch with us they'll run away, so my dad won't have to."

I laughed. "Smart and sneaky. I like it."

"What's your stance on Doctor Who?" he asked.

"If we're going to lay our geek cards on the table, I will tell you that I don't own a sonic screwdriver, but weeping angel statues freak me out."

"As they should." He stood. "I'm glad I ran into you today."

I was full of warm fuzzies. "Me, too."

He headed for his car. I sat there smiling like an idiot.

Aiden and Delia walked over, deep in conversation, or maybe they were arguing. It was hard to tell. Aiden stopped talking and glanced around. "Where's Grant?"

"He had to go rescue his dad from an awkward decorating situation."

"I guess I'll be going, too. See you at school," Aiden said, and then vanished practically like smoke.

"What is that about?" Delia stomped her foot. "Why does he bail as soon as Grant leaves?"

"Maybe he needs a wing-man in social situations." I popped up off the bench. "Let's go back to the house and bake. I have good news to share."

On the drive to my house I filled her in on my situation with Grant.

"That's awesome," Delia said.

"If Aiden is a follower, maybe he'll ask if you want date."

Delia rolled her eyes. "If the boy wants to ask me out, he better man up and do it. Otherwise he's being friend-zoned."

"Really?" I was surprised to hear this.

She nodded. "Now that Grant has figured out what he wants, I expect Aiden to do the same.

Chapter Eleven

Zoe

Grant and Aiden found Delia and me in the quad before classes started Monday morning.

"Hey." I smiled at him. "How was the Doctor Who marathon?"

"Good. How was the rest of your weekend?"

"Delia and I baked and went to the Art of Tea."

"So sorry I missed the looms."

"We could always make plans to go there after school," I teased.

"I'm sure you have to make special reservations for the looms," Grant said. "People are probably lined up waiting for a spot to open."

"Happily, the crochet corner has an open door policy. No reservations needed."

"I'll keep that in mind."

Out of the corner of my eye, I saw my brother glaring in my direction. I knew it wouldn't take long for him to hear about Grant and I being more than friends, but I thought I might have a slight grace period before the lectures started.

"Want me to go tell him I'm not trying to make you the Ringer?" Grant asked.

"That has bad idea written all over it." My brother's temper matched my own. It was best to let him get over the initial boil of anger and talk to him when he'd settled down to a low simmer.

My brother wasn't the only person giving us sideways glances. Lena came toward us with an odd smile on her face. She must have had a makeover because she'd gone from princess perfect ponytail to a girl who looked like she could star in a movie.

"Sorry to interrupt," she said. "Grant, I lost an earring at your house yesterday, would you look around and see if you can find it?"

Funny. He hadn't mentioned that Lena had been at his house yesterday.

"Sure. What's it look like?"

"Actually, it's one of the gold and silver hoops you gave me for Christmas last year."

He nodded. "Right. I'll let you know if it turns up."

"Thanks." She walked off like all eyes were upon her. And most of them were, although I was probably the only one glaring daggers at her.

Grant cleared his throat. "That was awkward."

"She probably left the earring at your place on purpose."

"Really?"

I nodded. "It gave her a reason to talk to you."

"That's weird."

A light bulb went off in my brain. "Was her visit the reason you came to see me?"

"What? I didn't come to see you."

"Please. I'd bet my house and Betty's Burgers are the only two places you've been to that far off the highway."

"Maybe."

I bumped him with my hip. "You ran away from her and toward me. I'm flattered."

The bell for class rang, and he walked me to first hour. Once I was seated, I braced myself for an attack from Lena that never came. Maybe she had finally moved on.

On the drive home from school Jack started in on me again.

"Zoe, what the hell are you doing with Grant?"

"We're dating. It's not a big deal."

"You're smarter than this. Can't you see what he's doing?" He smacked the steering wheel. "You're going to be the biggest joke at school."

"He's not trying to make me the Ringer." I believed this. Why couldn't my brother?

"Think about this whole situation logically. Why else would he date you?"

His words were like a punch in the gut. "Excuse me?"

"I'm being honest. He can have any girl he wants. Why would he choose you?"

I blinked back angry tears. "Why wouldn't he choose me? I'm cute. I'm funny."

"Yeah, you are, but you're not anything special," he stated like it was obvious.

I gasped for breath. It felt like a ten-ton weight sat on my chest. "I can't believe you said that to me. You're my brother. You're supposed to have my back."

"I'm trying to protect you. What's more likely? Him making you the Ringer to get back at me, or him thinking you're the hottest girl at Wilton?"

"Go to hell." I had no delusions that I was the hottest girl at school, or the smartest, or the prettiest, but that didn't mean Grant didn't like me. One thing for sure, I was done with Jack.

Turning away from him, I stared out the passenger window. No matter what it took, tomorrow I would find a way to school which didn't involve my brother.

When he pulled into the driveway, I practically ran from the car and pounded up the front steps. My grandmother looked up from the stove where she was cooking. "What's wrong?"

Jack slammed the door as he entered the house. "Zoe, I know you think I'm being a dick, but I'm trying to protect you."

"I'm not talking to you." I dropped my backpack on the kitchen chair and poured myself a glass of milk.

My grandmother turned the burner on low. "Jack, what did you do?"

Before he could get a word out I paraphrased his unbelievably rude comments.

"Jack Cain, no wonder your sister is upset. I know you have a past with this young man, but that's all it is—a past. You two boys probably butt heads because you're too much alike. And don't you ever tell your sister she isn't special. While the women in our family have never been super models, we are a smart, good-looking bunch."

Jack shook his head. "I swear Zoe, it's like you're standing on the train tracks and I can see the engine coming yet you refuse to acknowledge it."

"No matter how badly he worded it, your brother is trying to look out for you," my grandmother said.

"And it's not like there's anyone else around to do it," Jack said, his voice dropping as he spoke.

And guilt rained down on my head. "Is that why you're doing this...because Dad isn't here?"

Jack shrugged. "It's my job to look out for you. That's what I'm trying to do."

I blinked back tears. "I get it, but try trusting me a little."

"And you're not the only one looking out for her." My grandmother walked over and hugged Jack. It was weird to see that he was taller than her now. She stepped away and held him at arm's length. "And I do appreciate your effort, but give your sister some credit. She's a smart girl."

He nodded and backed away from my grandmother, heading for his bedroom. My grandmother returned to the stove and slowly stirred the pot. "Your brother is probably just being over-protective, but keep in mind that you don't know this Grant very well. He could be a good guy, but even good teenage boys can be trouble."

...

Since Jack had explained why he'd acted like such a jerk, I mostly forgave him. We settled on a we'll-agree-to-disagree policy where we didn't talk about Grant. That week, on the drive to and from school, we managed to avoid all talk of dating, but Friday morning, Jack was too quiet...suspiciously quiet. "Now you're making me nervous. Say something. Just make sure it's something nice."

"That's the problem." A bug splatted against the windshield. He turned on the wipers to clean it off. "There's a ton of stuff I want to say, but all of it will tick you off, and you probably won't believe me anyway."

I laughed. "Here I thought you might be ready to trust me."

"I trust you with a lot of things. Being around guys like Grant isn't one of them. Why can't you pick a normal guy?"

As we pulled into the parking lot, I realized it was time to remind him of some key facts. "It's your fault I kissed Grant in the first place. If you hadn't tried to boss me around, I never would have done it."

"I tried to warn you away from trouble and you dove in head first just to spite me."

I was beginning to wish he'd remained silent. "You didn't try to warn me, you gave me an ultimatum. How did you think I'd react?"

He pulled into a spot and parked. "Maybe I thought you'd be reasonable instead of acting like a brat throwing a tantrum."

"The only reason you don't like Grant is because you've lost out to him in the past. He's lost out to you, too. Why can't you get over it?"

"Do you remember, Katy, the girl I dated for about a month last year?"

I nodded. "I liked her."

"So did I. On the nights I had to work, when she went out with her friends, she kept running into Grant. After a few weeks, she dumped me to date him."

Wait a minute. "I thought Grant was with Lena last year."

"He was. That didn't stop him from dating Katy."

I couldn't picture Grant as the type who'd cheat on his girlfriend. Even someone as annoying as Lena. "You know this how?"

"One of Katy's friends told me. Apparently, he'd hang out with Katy whenever Lena wasn't available, but he never asked her on a real date. I'd bet money that he plans to do the exact same thing to you. He'll spend time with you, but he'll never ask you on a real date. So even if he isn't trying to make you the Ringer, that's how he's going to treat you. Guaranteed."

He was out of the car before I could tell him he was wrong, because Grant planned to take me to the school dance. I wasn't just someone to hang around with until something better came along, I was sure of it.

A tiny voice of doubt cropped up in my head. What if I was wrong? I hated that Jack made me doubt my own instincts and left me feeling insecure. Needing to bolster my confidence, I used the visor mirror to check my appearance. I looked a little pale. Some lip gloss should fix that. I grabbed the cherry gloss from by backpack and dabbed it on my lips.

Knock knock knock.

Startled, I jerked the lip gloss across my cheek.

Male laughter had me pushing the door open ready for a fight.

Grant's eyebrows went up. "You can't be mad about lip gloss."

I used the back of my hand to wipe the pink goo off my cheek. "No. I was mad at Jack before you startled me."

"Sorry." He reached out and rubbed his thumb near the corner of my mouth. "Missed a spot."

"Thanks." I gave a fake grin. "All better?"

"Yes." He glanced in the direction my brother had gone. "What did your brother do now?"

"You know what? It doesn't matter. My next priority is to find Delia because she should have a cup of coffee waiting for me."

Grant made a face like he smelled rotten eggs. "I don't know how you guys drink that stuff."

"You don't like coffee?" I placed a hand over my heart. "That's it. My image of you as the ideal male is shattered."

He shook his head. "Coffee breath is bad. Kissing someone with coffee breath is worse."

And suddenly I knew how I could turn my day around and prove to myself that Grant cared. Moving in close, I played with his tie. "Maybe you should kiss me before I drink any."

I smiled up at him, expecting him to lean down and kiss me, but he just stood there. He didn't lean down. He didn't even react. He acted like I wasn't there. Ouch. My face heated. Tears stung my eyes. I dropped his tie and stumbled back a step.

Keeping my eyes on the ground, I dodged around him and headed toward the quad. I needed Delia, now.

"Zoe, wait," Grant called after me.

Not going to happen. There's only so much rejection a girl can take before eight a.m., and I'd had my quota. Speeding up, I made a beeline toward the area where Delia and I usually hung out. And my rotten luck continued. No pink hair in sight. I scanned the quad and came up empty. Where was she?

"You walk fast for a short person." Grant's voice came from behind me.

"Thanks for pointing that out." I didn't turn around, because making eye contact with Grant right now could be fatal. If he looked at me with disinterest, or worse, pity, the tears I'd held back were going to make a break for it. "Can you see Delia anywhere?"

"No. Zoe...turn around."

"Sorry. My grandma says bad things come in threes. And I'd prefer that number three not come from you." And with that, I headed for the cafeteria to grab a cup of coffee. With every step, I replayed the scene in the parking lot. We'd been talking. He'd acted like he cared about why I was upset. He touched my face. He could've said, "Hey, moron, you have lip gloss on your cheek." But he hadn't. So why didn't he want to kiss me? Did he not want to kiss me at all anymore? That would suck.

"Earth to Zoe." Delia appeared by my side carrying two cups of coffee. "Geez, what were you thinking about?"

"Coffee." I took the cup she offered and swallowed half of it in one gulp.

"Right. That's why you look like you're going to snap and kill someone."

Grabbing her arm I dragged her over to a less crowded area and gave her a rundown of my morning's humiliation.

"Wow. Jack is more of a tool than I realized, and Grant is a dumb ass."

"That about sums it up."

"As your grandma would say, watch out for number three."

"Exactly."

...

First hour passed by without Lena making a single comment. She wore a strange smile, which in my emotionally heightened state made me wonder what she was plotting and simultaneously made me want to punch her in the nose. When class ended, she said, "Smile. You're going to be famous."

"What?"

She laughed and walked away.

My stomach plummeted to my feet. I knew without a doubt that an amused Lena meant bad things for me.

"Crap." I heard Delia mutter. My classmates were laughing about something on their phones.

"Follow me," Delia said. "And act like nothing is wrong."

And that meant something was very, very wrong. My heart rate sped up and my palms began to sweat. Knowing Delia would help, I followed her to the girls' bathroom. On the way, everyone seemed to whisper and point at me. What the hell?

Once we were locked in a bathroom stall, Delia handed me her phone, open to YouTube. "I'm sorry. Number three just hit."

On the screen, my epic fail played for all to see. I was smiling up at Grant, expecting him to kiss me and he totally blew me off. He was acting like he didn't even know or care I was standing there. There I was, for all to see, stumbling away, with my face bright red.

No. No. No. No. No. I shoved the phone back at Delia. This could not be happening. Prickly heat broke out on my skin. Cold sweat coated my forehead. Breathe in. Breathe out. Breathe in. Breathe out. Puking in the stall at school where everyone would hear about it ten seconds after it happened was not an option.

"I'd bet a million bucks Lena posted it," Delia said.

"What am I going to do? Everyone's going to see it."

"I think they've already seen it. It's not that bad." Delia shoved the phone back in her pocket. "Besides, I'm sure Grant will hunt you down to diffuse the situation, because he knows you aren't a suffer-in-silence kind of girl. Maybe you could use this to your advantage."

I didn't know what she meant, and I didn't have time to figure it out. We barely made it to our next class on time. People stared; I gritted my teeth, and gave everyone my best I don't give a shit what you think smile.

My jaw ached by the time lunch rolled around. I wasn't sure if I could eat. A large bowl of ice cream might work. People stared and whispered as Delia and I entered the cafeteria. Pride kept my head up and my shoulders back. I would not cower. I might get sick to my stomach and break out in a cold sweat—check and check—but I would not run and hide.

I spotted Lena sitting at a table surrounded by other girls, laughing and talking. My hands curled into fists. "How many detentions would I get for punching someone in the face?"

"As much as I'd love to find out, we're not going to play that way." Delia led me over to a table in the center of the room.

"Why are we sitting here?" I didn't want to be on display like this.

"To show people you don't care." Delia set her back pack down. "I'm starving today."

What was up with the loud voice?

"Your turn." She laughed, like she'd made a joke. "Act like nothing's wrong and it will drive Lena crazy."

As plans went, this one pretty much sucked but it wasn't like I had any better ideas. So, I smiled and laughed as we walked up to the buffet. Once we were in line, I said, "Hey, look, they have chicken tenders today." "Yum." Delia loaded up her plate.

I could feel everyone staring at me. My face heated, but I kept up the act. "What sounds really good right now, is the lemon meringue pie from Betty's."

Delia made a sound that was borderline obscene, causing several guys at the buffet to turn and stare. "What? The lemon meringue pie at Betty's is awesome."

And now I was laughing for real. If I made it through this day, I would buy Delia her own pie, for being the best friend ever.

Back at the table, I ate chicken tenders without tasting them, and kept up the fake conversation with Delia.

When there was ten minutes of lunch left, I said, "Notice who's not eating lunch here today?"

"No Grant, and no Aiden. Makes you wonder what they're up to."

"Exactly." Where were they? Shouldn't Grant be worried about how I was dealing with all this crap?

"It's kind of cowardly," Delia said, "leaving you to deal with this alone."

"Sad, but true. Maybe I'll spill something on him in Foods class, or accidentally stab him with a knife."

And I might have stabbed him, given a chance, but he wasn't in Foods class. Where the heck was he?

Chapter Twelve

Zoe

Ms. Ida didn't ask the class where Grant was, so she must have known he wasn't coming. I made cinnamon streusel muffins by myself while compulsively checking the classroom door, waiting for the object of my affection to come in so I could rip his head off. No such luck.

After class, I hung behind while the room cleared out.

"Ms. Ida, do you know where Grant is?"

"He signed out for a family emergency," Ms. Ida said.

Family emergency my ass. Grinding my teeth, I headed for my next class. That jerk had left me here to deal with this by myself. The next time I saw him he was a dead man.

I was halfway to my class when a boy with teeth too big for his fake smile blocked my path. "Hello, Zoe."

"Hi." What did this guy want?

"I'm Phin." He gave me more of his off-balance smile. The guy should model for toothpaste commercials.

"Nice to meet you." I tried to dodge by him, but he moved with me. "Phin, I need to go to class."

"My family has more money than the Evertides." He ran his hand down my arm in a way that made me want to run and take a shower.

"How nice for you. Now get out of my way." I pulled my backpack off and held it in front of me so he couldn't get too close.

And then he winked at me and backed up a few steps. "We'll talk later."

"No. We won't." Weirded out, I ran to class, barely making it to my seat before the bell rang.

Lena smirked at me from her seat across the room. I fantasized about slamming her face into the desk, repeatedly.

By the end of the day, I felt like a slingshot someone had pulled back but forgotten to release. On the way to meet Jack at the car, Phin popped up again.

"There you are." He gave me that smile again. Did he really think that was a good look?

I walked past him, figuring I wouldn't encourage him. A hand grabbed my arm, and I jerked to a stop. Whipping around I yanked my arm from his grasp. "Back off."

"Whoa." He held both hands up and laughed.

"Whatever it is you want, I'm not interested. Go away." There. I couldn't be any clearer.

His smile tightened, and his eyes turned hard and mean. "That wasn't very nice."

The hair on the back of my neck stood up. Something about this guy was off. Backing away from him, I said, "Nothing personal. I hate all guys right now." And then I spun around and headed to the car, where Jack stood watching me.

Once we were on the highway, Jack said, "From Grant, to Phin, you sure know how to pick them."

"I didn't pick Phin. I was trying to get away from him." I wiped my sweat coated palms on my skirt. "Thanks for the help."

"How am I supposed to know which assholes you want to talk to and which ones you don't?"

"For the sake of argument, let's say Grant is the only snob I want to talk to. If you see some other jerk grabbing at me, come help."

He was silent for a moment. "Sorry. I'll tell him to leave you alone."

"Thanks. Speaking of my life going to hell, did you see the video?"

"I did, but I wasn't going to say anything."

Huh. "Is that because you didn't want to upset me, or because you like what the video means?"

"Both. Want me to stop at Betty's for a pie on the way home?"

I laughed. "Yes, and now I believe you really do care about me."

...

The weekend passed with no word from Grant. What had I expected? He didn't owe me anything. He wasn't the one who looked like an idiot on YouTube. I'd had to set my account to friends only, which I'd narrowed down to Delia, because guys were sending me pervy messages. Somehow Grant not kissing me made guys think I was open to kissing, or doing other things with them. What kind of stupid logic was that?

Sunday morning, my grandmother came into my room. "I heard about what happened at school Friday."

Great. I pulled the covers up over my head. "I'm staying under here until someone destroys the Internet."

She tugged the cover down from my face. "When I was a teenager, if you made a mistake, everyone teased you for a while and then forgot. The internet makes that more difficult."

"Can you home-school me?" I asked, only half joking.

"No, but I can help you get over this." She patted my leg.

"Come on. Let's go shoot cans off the back fence." It was better than nothing.

...

When Monday morning rolled around, I wanted to lie on the kitchen floor and throw a fit like a toddler. I settled for saying, "I don't want to go to school."

My mom downed her coffee and checked the clock. "I'm sorry, sweetie. You have to keep moving forward. One foot in front of the other." She gave me the same pained smile she'd worn since Dad died.

"Okay, Mom."

"That's my girl." She patted me on the shoulder as she walked by.

My grandmother waited until Mom walked out the front door. "She can't help it, Zoe."

"I know." I swallowed over the lump in my throat. My mom had suffered serious depression after my dad died. Not like the rest of us hadn't, but when she came out of it there was something missing. Like she never came back all the way...she never really felt anything anymore, or seemed to care about any of us.

Right now I'd give a million dollars not to care about the stupid video.

The only bright spot in my morning was Delia promising to meet me in the parking lot with a cup of coffee so she could give me a pep talk before I faced the masses.

...

"I say we kneecap Lena, Grant, and Phin," Delia said as we sat in her truck drinking coffee.

"Sure, why not?" I took a deep breath and checked the lot for Grant's shiny black sports car. No luck. A ton of students milled about, like they were waiting for someone to make fun of. "I've changed my mind. I'm going to hide in your truck all day."

"Nope. We are wearing our big girl panties today and we're going to deal with this."

"How?" I threw my hands up in disgust. "Pretending it doesn't bother me is not the answer. It bothers me. It bothers me a lot. I'm not sure who I'm madder at, Lena for posting the video, or Grant for rejecting me and then leaving me to deal with the fallout by myself."

"Yeah, that was a dick move." She opened the truck door. "Let's go find him and cause a scene."

Oh, God. "How will that help?"

Delia strutted through the parking lot like she was the reigning queen. "It may not help, but it'll be fun."

"Can't we sit quietly on a bench somewhere?"

"No. As your best friend, it's my job to help you show everyone you don't give a crap what they think." We headed for the spot where Grant and Aiden normally hung out.

Aiden was there, but no Grant.

Delia marched up to him. "Where is he?"

Aiden adjusted his glasses and tilted his head. "He who?"

"You're too smart to play dumb," Delia said. "Where is Grant?"

"He's trying to solve a problem."

"And what problem would that be?" It better be my problem, or I was going to do something really ugly to the next person who messed with me.

Aiden hitched his backpack higher on his shoulder. "He's talking to Phin."

That was good. "Wait a minute. How did he know Phin was bothering me?"

"Phin has a big mouth." Aiden gave a tight smile.

"I'm sure I'll regret asking this, but what does that mean?"

Looking down at his shoes, Aiden cleared his throat. "Phin bragged that he'd make you the Ringer before Grant could."

"He's dead." Fists clenched, I whirled around looking for the idiot. His too large teeth in his obnoxious fake grin were nowhere in sight.

"Zoe." Grant's voice came from behind me.

I whipped around. "Where the hell have you been? Do you know the kind of crap I've been dealing with? Everyone is watching that stupid video, and Phin is stalking me."

"He won't bother you anymore."

"How do you know that?" My face was hot, and my eyes burned with angry tears.

"He works with my father, so I know certain things about his family he doesn't want everyone at Wilton to know. Believe me when I say, he won't come near you again."

I wanted to believe him. And I was grateful, but Phin was just the tip of the iceberg of the colossal mess my life had become. "And the video? Have you seen it?"

"Yes. People keep sending me links."

"Because of you, I'm going to have to transfer back to public school."

"This isn't all my fault," Grant said. "If you hadn't run off Friday morning, with your weird rule of three thing—"

I held up three fingers. "The video was number three."

"Whatever. If you'd talked to me instead of acting like a drama queen, I could've told you I saw Lena pointing her phone at us, which distracted me, so I didn't realize you were trying to kiss me until after you had run off."

Oh. My. God. "Why didn't you come find me and tell me that? Where did you go?"

"I wasn't here because my grandfather was rushed to the hospital."

And my anger deflated like a helium balloon the day after a party. "Is he all right?"

"He is now. It was something with his heart. They're running some tests."

"I'm sorry about your grandpa." And I was, but I was in the middle of my own crisis. "Back to Friday, are you saying you would've kissed me if you'd been paying attention?" I was setting myself up, and I knew it. I might as well give him a bat to smack me in the head with.

"I stopped to talk to you, didn't I?" Grant shoved his hand back through his hair. "I could have walked past your car."

Over Grant's shoulder, I saw girls pointing and snickering. "That makes me feel better, but everyone thinks you blew me off. Guys I don't know are sending me pervy messages. How are we going to fix this?"

"Better yet, how are we going to get revenge?" Delia asked.

"Catch Lena doing something stupid and put it on You Tube?" Aiden suggested.

Delia reached over and patted his arm. "You've redeemed yourself."

"I don't understand you." Aiden stared at her like she was a problem he couldn't solve.

"Ask me on a date and I'll give you a few clues," Delia said.

"We could go on a double date," Grant suggested. "That would show people I wasn't blowing you off."

Part of me wanted to jump up and down and celebrate, but the other part of me needed this humiliation taken care of right now. "Sure. I guess. But that doesn't change how everyone is looking at me now."

Grant tilted his head and studied me. "You guess you want to go on a date with me? You mean you're not sure?"

Was he trying to start a fight? "You know what I mean. A date would be nice, but it won't fix the big problem I'm having right this minute."

"A date would be nice." He crossed his arms over his chest. "Nice. That's what all guys strive for."

"Oh my God. Could you pull your head out of your ass for a minute and focus on the real issue here." And there was dead silence all around us. I cringed. "I said that a little loud, didn't I?"

Delia was biting her lip like she was trying not to laugh.

Aiden looked back and forth between Grant and me like he was waiting for something to explode.

Grant's eyes narrowed and he moved closer, putting his hand on my shoulder. "You want me to fix this right now?" His tone wasn't mad, but it had an edge that made me nervous.

Afraid of what might come out of my mouth if I opened it, I nodded.

"Fine." He wrapped his other arm around my waist, pulled my body flush against his, and kissed me. It was a no holds barred kiss like you see in the movies. Catcalls sounded in the background. There might have been some clapping. Not that I cared.

"Mr. Evertide," a voice thundered.

Grant stepped away from me and turned to face a teacher I didn't know. "Yes?"

"Detention for both of you."

Grant pointed at me. "She started it." My jaw dropped, and then I laughed.

The teacher did not appear amused. "Report to the principal's office after school."

"Will do." Grant put his arm around my shoulders.

"Happy?"

"Yes." And I was.

"All done," Delia said.

"What's all done?" I asked.

Delia passed me her phone. On her You Tube page there was a video of Grant kissing me, with the caption: *Suck on that, Lena.*

Chapter Thirteen

Zoe

After school, Grant and I headed to the principal's office together. Unlike last detention, we were ushered into Principal Stephens's office, where he waited for us behind his desk like he was holding court. There were chairs but he didn't tell us to sit.

"If there's another incident of this nature between you two I will be forced to call in your parents. You know where to go." He waved us toward the door. We made a quick exit and headed over to the table where we'd sat before. By the frown on the secretary's face, I could tell her demeanor hadn't improved. She pulled out the chicken timer, twisted its head around with a little too much enthusiasm, and then ignored us.

Since we were stuck I figured I might as well get some homework done. I could feel Grant staring at me while I did my math problems. Should I look up and smile at him? Maybe, maybe not. Let him wonder what I'm thinking, for a change. In my mind, I was mentally skipping through a field full of flowers, singing, He likes me. He likes me. He really, really likes me. In reality, I decided to keep things a little more low key.

Kissing me like that, on the quad in front of everyone, made us look like we were a couple. Something he claimed he didn't want. So, my plan was to avoid any sort of relationship or girlfriend/boyfriend type talk. I could do cool and controlled, now that I knew he cared enough to land himself in detention to save my sanity.

It took forever for the dead chicken timer to go off.

When it did, I casually packed up my bag and headed for the door. No clingy girl here. Nope. Just a cool girl who liked a guy who was taking her on a real date this weekend.

"What are you smiling about?" Grant opened the office door for me.

"Detention is over. I finished my homework. Life is good."

"Doesn't take much to make you happy, does it?" He checked his cell as we walked down the hall. "I need to make a stop before I take you home. Is that all right?"

"Sure. Where are we going?"

"My grandfather wants me to pick up a book for him."

We took the door which led to the side parking lot. Cold crisp air swirled leaves in mini tornadoes on the ground.

"What kind of book does he want?"

"He collects first editions of the classics. Something he's been waiting for came in at Bibliophiles."

"I'm guessing that's some sort of bookstore."

"Brilliant deduction, Sherlock." He pulled out his key fob and pressed the button, which made the shiny black sports car beep and flash its lights.

"Is it one of those bookstores that has a cafe in it where I can buy an obscenely large cookie and a mocha latte?"

"No."

I pouted, hoping he'd take the hint.

He shook his head and laughed. "Fine. We'll get food. But we're not eating in my car."

Bibliophiles was like no other bookstore I'd ever seen. Most of the books were in locked cases. Those books that were set out on shelves had leather covers with the title stamped on the spine in gold ink. "I'm guessing they don't have the latest New York Times bestsellers."

"No. And it's best if you don't touch anything."

I would've been offended if there was anything in the place I wanted to touch. While we stood at a counter in the back of the store, I peered around, searching for a price tag poking out from one of the books. None were visible which reminded me of the adage, "If you have to ask, you can't afford it."

A man in a suit greeted Grant and then disappeared into the back of the store and came out with a book wrapped in clear plastic. "The Mylar cover protects the book from your touch. Please handle it carefully, and keep it out of the sun."

A book you weren't supposed to touch. That was a new one.

Grant accepted the book like it was a glass sculpture. "Thank you. I know my grandfather will love it."

I had a weird thought that in the future these books would be mementos of Grant's grandfather. Books were nice, but I preferred something I could wear or keep with me all the time, like my watch.

Once we exited the store, I had two questions. "Where are we going now, and when do we get to the food part?"

Grant's cell signaled that he had a text. He checked the screen and frowned. "My grandfather wants me to bring the book to him now." He stared down the street. "There's a deli nearby. I could drop you there and then come back after I see him."

Was he trying to ditch me? "You don't want me to go with you?"

He blinked and looked at me like I was insane. "You said you were hungry. I was trying to be nice."

Lame excuse. "I don't want to eat by myself."

"Fine. You can come to the hospital with me."

And now the deli sounded like a good idea. "He's still in the hospital?"

"They're running tests before they send him home. It's no big deal."

Was he trying to convince himself or me? "Maybe I'll wait in the car while you run the book up to him."

"Suit yourself."

We drove to the hospital in silence. I told myself Grant was irritable because of his grandfather. His mood didn't have anything to do with me. Fifteen minutes later when we reached the parking lot of the small private hospital, I'd almost convinced myself it was true. Time to suck it up and be a better person.

"I can come in with you if you want company. Hospitals can be hard to take some times."

He turned the car off and sat there for a moment. "The last time I saw him, he was pale and hooked up to all these IVs."

"He must be feeling better if he wants his book." I squeezed Grant's hand.

As soon as we stepped foot in the hospital, the smell of antiseptic, fear, and desperation hit me. I hated that smell. Breathing through my mouth I concentrated on being there for Grant. This wasn't my tragedy.

When we reached his private room, Grant's grandfather sat in a chair flipping channels on a flat screen television.

"You're out of bed." Grant sounded relieved.

"I told you the doctors were worried over nothing." He spotted me and frowned. "Who's this?"

Great. He disapproved of me on sight.

"This is Zoe."

"You'll have to excuse my appearance." Grant's grandfather adjusted his robe. "I don't normally receive visitors in my pajamas."

"It's nice to meet you, anyway." I remembered something. "I think you went to school with my grandmother, Monica Brooks."

His eyes narrowed, and then there was a spark of recognition. "She was a lovely girl."

The nurse came in. "Sorry to break this up, but it's time for your grandfather to prove he's ready to go home. We're going to walk the stairs."

"I'm up for the challenge, my dear." Grant's grandfather smiled at the nurse.

"I'll put the book in your overnight bag." Grant reverently tucked the book in his grandfather's suitcase. On the way out the door, he stopped and took his grandfather's hand. "Glad to see you're feeling better."

"You and me both."

...

Zoe

The week settled into a comfortable routine. Grant and Aiden ate lunch with Delia and me every day, but they never mentioned the upcoming date.

"Why haven't they said anything?" I asked Delia Thursday afternoon as we carried our trays across the cafeteria to the table where Aiden and Grant already sat.

"I don't know."

"We need to know what's going on." It was driving me crazy. "I'm going to ask them."

"Maybe we should give them time to say something first. Aiden is like a frightened rabbit reaching for a carrot. I don't want to startle him away."

"What part of you is a carrot?" I asked.

She laughed. "Yeah, that didn't come out like I thought it would. New plan. You ask and I'll play back-up."

"Works for me." When we reached the lunch table I sat next to Grant. "So where are we going on our double date tomorrow?"

He blinked, like he could have cared less. "I hadn't thought about it."

Not the answer I'd hoped for. I glanced at Delia, signaling she was up to bat.

"Have you thought about our date?" she asked Aiden.

He froze for a second. The rabbit metaphor was beginning to make more sense.

"My first response was going to be no." Aiden studied Delia. "But I'm pretty sure that's the wrong answer. So where would you like to go?"

"Well done." Delia congratulated him. "We could go to a movie."

Grant's cell buzzed. He checked a text and frowned.

"Who's that from?" I leaned in, but he'd turned off the screen.

"No one important."

Why didn't he want me to know who texted him? "Then why did you turn it off so fast?"

He pulled his phone out and handed it to me. "See for yourself."

I should have handed him the phone back, not caring who texted, but I wasn't that mature. Instead, I clicked on messages. Amber had invited him to a party. She'd added one of those stupid blowing kisses smiley faces. I gripped the phone tighter and checked the texting history. Ten messages came up from the past week. What the hell did she think she was doing? Amber chasing after him set the short fuse of my temper on a slow burn but I wouldn't play the jealous girlfriend.

"Nice smiley faces. The next time I text you, maybe I should use fluffy pink bunnies."

"From you, I'd expect shotguns or hedge clippers."

...

Friday I met up with Delia and we went to the same spot where we'd met up with Aiden and Grant every morning this week. When Aiden spotted Delia, he smiled, like he was happy to see her. Grant didn't notice my approach because he was talking to Amber. And she was touching him. She brushed her fingers across his arm as she talked to him. On the positive side, he stepped away from her. When he did, he caught sight of me and rolled his eyes.

She didn't notice. Instead, she moved closer and touched his shoulder.

Why wasn't Amber taking the hint? Should I tell her to get away from my boyfriend? Not that Grant was my boyfriend. He was just a guy I was going on a date with, or according to my brother, he was a guy trying to humiliate me in front of the whole school by making me the Ringer. I hated that Jack had planted that thought in my head.

Since saying anything about a relationship would be awkward, I decided to go with a more direct approach.

"Excuse me," I said to Amber right before I squeezed between her and Grant, threw my arms around his neck and kissed him. At first, he seemed surprised, but he caught on to the idea soon enough.

"Miss Cain," an authoritative voice called out.

Busted. I moved away from Grant and turned to see my first hour teacher, Mr. Fletcher.

"You know the rules."

"Detention for both of us?" I asked.

He nodded and walked off.

Grant sighed.

I grinned at him. "Sorry, had to be done."

Amber muttered something under her breath and stalked off.

The day flew by. Before I knew it, I was in the principal's office standing next to Grant. Principal Stephens was packing a briefcase. "You two are lucky. I don't have time to call your parents today. In lieu of that punishment, I want you to write sentences during detention."

He shoved two pieces of paper at Grant. "You know where to go."

We shuffled over to the table. Grant handed me one of the sheets of paper. At the top was written "Principal Stephens will call my parents if I end up at this table again."

Who knew the man had a sense of humor? It didn't say how many times he wanted us to copy the sentence, so I wrote at a leisurely pace waiting for the dead chicken timer to go off. When it did, I tried to hand the sentences to the secretary.

"Why would I want those?" she said.

Okay. The woman needed some happy pills.

It took every ounce of self-control I possessed not to bug Grant about where we were going on our date. By the time we made it to his car, I was ready to burst.

"I'm impressed." Grant opened the car door for me.

I slid into his low slung sports car, holding my backpack on my lap so I wouldn't flash him. "Impressed about what?"

"You haven't asked about the date." He said this like he knew it was killing me and then walked around the car.

I let him start the car and put it in drive, before I commented. "What are we going to do?"

"Now that I think about it, detention and the ride home should count as the date. So once I drop you off, I'll go home, call Aiden and see what he wants to do."

"Faulty logic and bad plan." I punched him on the shoulder. "Besides, Delia would not be pleased, and you don't want us plotting against you."

"I hate to tell you this, but you're not that scary." Grant pulled onto the highway. The speedometer needle edged above seventy.

"One, you're speeding and two, you have no idea how scary we can be."

He eased off the gas. "Right. What have you done?"

I grinned at one of my fondest memories. "You can't repeat this to anyone. Understand?"

"Got it."

"When we were kids, Delia and I set up a lemonade stand at the Fields Cross baseball diamond. Jack told everyone he peed in the lemonade, so no one bought any."

"Did he pee in the lemonade?"

"I wasn't going to drink it and find out because he might have. So, Delia and I didn't sell anything, and we'd spent days painting signs and drawing on all the paper cups. That night, when we went back to my house, we put Nair in Jack's shampoo bottle. The next morning, he took a shower and came out bald. No hair, no eyebrows, nothing. It was awesome."

He sucked in a breath. "Ouch."

I laughed. "It took him a month to grow back enough hair so that he could stop wearing a hat."

"So the moral of this story is, I have to keep our double date or I'll end up bald?"

"Pretty much, so what do you want to do tonight?" A movie sounded good to me, after everything else that happened today, I wanted to be low maintenance.

"Do you like air hockey?" he asked.

"Yes." I rocked at air hockey but he didn't need to know that.

"Let's go to Edison's."

Edison's was a combination restaurant and arcade, which had laser tag and video games. "That could be fun as long as you're not one of those guys who has to win every game all the time. Because I like to win, too."

"I could throw a few games for you." He turned off onto the road, which led back to my house.

"I could do the same for you."

"Right. I don't think that will be necessary."

Four hours later, I stood in the kitchen in front of my grandma and mom, showing off my outfit of an off the shoulder sweater my good butt jeans and black heels. Jack refused to acknowledge me, but he muttered under his breath a lot.

"What do you think?" I asked.

"You look hot," my grandmother said.

"Mother." My mom sighed.

"What? Do you want her to go out dressed like an old lady?" Grandma asked.

"You're looking pretty good yourself, Grandma. Where are you going?"

She straightened the collar of her black wrap dress. "Thank you. I'm helping out at the silent auction for the garden club tonight."

I wiggled my eyebrows. "Grandma's on the prowl."

"We'll see." She said. "Maybe Everett will be there."

Gross. "You can't date Grant's grandpa. That would be weird."

"Cancel your date, and stop acting like an idiot and it won't be a problem," my brother shouted from the living room.

"Jack, stop giving your sister such a hard time," my mother called out.

Yeah. Like saying that to him accomplished anything. The sound of a car coming up the drive had me darting to the window. A beige Volvo sat in the driveway. Had to be Aiden's car.

The back door opened and Grant climbed out looking amazing in dark jeans and an emerald green shirt. And he'd caught me gaping at him through the window. Great. Way to play it cool.

I wanted to rush the door, but let my grandma open it instead. "Hello, I'm Zoe's grandmother. You must be Grant."

"Nice to meet you."

"Just so you know, those shotguns are real." My grandmother pointed to the back wall where the weapons hung above the mantle.

Grant's smile faltered. "Okay."

"Grandma." I couldn't believe she'd done that. I half ran to the door, before anyone said anything else to ruin my date. "See you guys later."

Grant's gaze went to my exposed shoulders.

"I saw that," my grandma said.

Chapter Fourteen

Zoe

"Go." I pushed Grant out of the doorway onto the porch. "Let's make a run for it before this becomes awkward."

"Too late." Grant put his hand on my arm and we headed for the car.

Heat from his hand seeped through my sweater, warming my skin. When we reached the car, he opened the door for me. I climbed in, but wasn't sure if I was supposed to climb over to the other side, or if he was going to walk around the car and get in from that side. Why did life suddenly seem so complicated? When he shut my door I had the answer.

Delia turned around and said, "Nice sweater."

I pointed at Delia's hair. "Nice purple streaks. I think I like them better than the pink."

"I had the matching eye liner, so I figured I'd give it a shot." Delia jerked her thumb toward Aiden. "I don't think he likes the new me."

"I never said I didn't like it. I asked why you did it."

The reason was obvious to me. She'd done it to mess with Aiden's head. "Should I tell him why?" I asked Delia.

"No," Aiden and Delia said at the same time.

We all looked at Aiden. "What?" he said. "I like to figure things out for myself."

...

Edison's parking lot was packed. What would it be like inside?

"Grant, did you call to see if there was a birthday party here tonight?" Aiden asked.

"No."

"They have parties here all the time. What's the big deal?" I said. "Maybe we can scam some cake."

Aiden pulled into a spot in the row farthest from the building and turned the car off. "You can't take someone else's birthday cake."

"Sure you can," I said. "Everyone buys one of those monster sheet cakes, and there's always some left over which they have to lug home. If I take a piece of cake, I'm helping."

"You can't believe that." Grant opened his door and climbed out.

"Wrong," I said. "I can believe whatever I want."

The four of us trekked across the parking lot. Inside Edison's we were surrounded by a sea of little kids. Aiden froze. "Maybe we should go to the movies."

Grant leaned in close and whispered, "Little kids make him nervous because they're unpredictable."

Delia pointed toward the restaurant side of the establishment. "Come on. We'll hide out in a booth over there, and they'll probably be gone by the time we're finished eating."

Seated in the booth, Aiden appeared less stressed. The waitress came and took our order, and then Aiden pointed to Delia's paint striped skirt. "Are you the artist?"

Delia nodded.

Aiden tilted his head like he was thinking. "You made your skirt. Is that what you want to do, design clothes?"

"I love to design all sorts of things."

"Delia and I plan to open an eclectic boutique where she can sell clothes and artsy stuff while I sell cookies and cupcakes," I volunteered.

"Wouldn't it make more sense to open a normal bakery?" Grant said. "I mean there is a reason they don't let you take food into most stores."

His dismissal of my dream job ticked me off. "We want to create something different. We aren't shooting for normal."

He blinked. "Why do you sound upset? We're just having a conversation."

"No," I said, "you used the 'implied idiot.'"

Grant frowned. "You lost me."

"Your comment implies I'm stupid about business. So you pretty much called me an idiot, even if you didn't say it."

"That may be what you heard, but that's not what I meant." Grant paused for a moment. "Let's rewind this conversation and I'll try again. That's an interesting idea."

"You can rewind conversations?" I kind of liked the idea.

"If you can revoke freak outs, I can rewind conversations." He looked at me like he was daring me to argue.

"That works for me."

"Here we go, one extra-large pepperoni pizza." The waitress set the pizza down in the center of the table. "Is there anything else I can get you?"

"No. We're good." And we were. Grant's rewinding comment had dissolved the tension that had sprung up between us. I grabbed the spatula and put a piece of pizza on my plate and then passed it to Grant.

"New topic. What games do you like to play?" I asked Grant.

"Air hockey and anything where I get to shoot a gun or make things explode."

I laughed. "I love House of the Dead."

"I didn't think girls liked games like that."

"I like shooting guns and making things explode too, but I don't like the ones where you kill people."

"Zombies are people," Aiden said.

"No they're not." I shook parmesan cheese onto my pizza. "They used to be people, now they're the undead. So it's okay to shoot them and watch their heads explode."

Grant choked on his pizza, almost spitting food across the table. Delia laughed.

"What do you like to play?" Aiden asked Delia.

"I like foosball."

"Why do you like foosball? And before you pull a Zoe, there is no implied anything. I just ask a lot of questions because I like to understand things."

Chapter Fifteen

Zoe

For the rest of the meal, we kept to safe small talk about school and the games we wanted to play. Once the table was cleared, Grant pointed toward the air hockey tables. "Let's start over there."

Time to show off my air hockey skills.

Grant pulled an Edison's card from his wallet and swiped it through the scanner. "You know how to play?"

"First to seven points wins?"

He nodded and slapped the puck. I deflected it and sent it sailing back to his side of the table. He blocked my attempt at a goal and slammed it toward me where it smacked into my goal. The buzzer went off announcing he'd won a point. I groaned. Grant chuckled.

Time to wipe the smile off of his face. I served the puck bouncing it off the corner of the table in the exact angle to slide into his goal. The buzzer went off. His mouth fell open. "You lied to me."

"I did not." I set my paddle in a defensive position while he served. "You never asked if I was good at air hockey. You asked if I liked it."

"Now you sound like Aiden."

I checked to see where Delia and Aiden were.

Smack.

The buzzer went off. He'd scored another goal.

"Hey, that's cheating. I wasn't ready."

"Did you call a time out?" he asked.

"No." I smacked the puck sending it flying toward his goal. He blocked and ricocheted the puck off the right wall. I slapped it back to him hitting the corner of his goal. He blocked. Back and forth, we went point for point until we reached six-all. Winded, I held the puck. "Time out. I need a break."

"You're delaying the inevitable." He leaned over the table, guarding his goal.

His dark hair fell in waves across his forehead. His blue eyes shone like he knew victory was moments away. And he was smirking at me. I was caught between wanting to kiss him or whacking him upside the head with my paddle.

"And it all comes down to the final point," I said in a mock sportscaster voice. Setting the puck down, I smashed it across the table. He whacked it back toward me. I blocked. It ricocheted toward his goal. He blocked and smacked it diagonally, going for a slap shot. I blocked, and it ricocheted in the opposite direction, sliding into my goal. The buzzer went off.

"No." I threw my head back. "I want a rematch."

He spun his paddle in his hand, smiling in a way which made my heart beat faster. "Maybe later. Right now, I want to shoot zombies."

I wanted him to kiss me. But I didn't say that out loud. I pretended to pout. "Fine."

On the way across the room, he put his arm around my waist, guiding me through the crowd.

For the next ten minutes, we shot the living dead. And I was a better shot. Which I refrained from pointing out. After ten minutes of play we both died. The scores came up on the screen, and I had beaten him by 15,000. Jumping up and down, I said, "Woo hoo. I won."

Someone bumped into me. Off balance, I careened into Grant's chest. "Sorry. Maybe these weren't the best shoes to wear."

His gaze traveled down to my shoes and back up again. "I like the shoes."

I was three seconds from launching myself at his lips. He grinned like he knew what I was thinking. He pointed toward the guy's restroom. "I'm going to make a pit stop and then I think we should go outside and get some air."

Waiting by the House of the Dead Game, I imagined all the possible ways the date could go from here. Air? Did that mean let's kiss on the patio? Or did that mean he was warm? Yet another question in the minefield of dating. Some girl should write a guide deciphering all the things guys say.

Grant returned from the restroom with an odd expression on his face, like he was confused. He didn't say anything, so I didn't ask. He held my hand as we headed out the side door where Edison's had patio tables, chairs, and benches. Chillbumps broke out on my skin. Instinct told me to move closer to Grant, to share his body heat. But, I didn't want to seem too eager. Stupid, I know. Like he hadn't figured out I wanted to kiss him.

Another shiver ran through me, and this time Grant put his arm around my shoulders. Yay me.

Couples sat at tables talking or kissing. Actually most of the couples were kissing. In my head I did a small happy dance. Grant wanted to kiss me. He headed toward an unoccupied bench. We sat, and he kept his arm around me, but he didn't lean in like he planned to kiss me. Instead, he said, "I think Delia and Aiden going on a date was a mistake."

What? I stared at him trying to figure out what was going on, because A. He wasn't kissing me. B. He wanted to talk about our friends. Wow. Maybe the off the shoulder sweater didn't work for me after all.

Once my brain re-engaged, I said, "Why do you say that?"

"He probably sees her as a puzzle to solve. I don't think he's interested in someone like Delia."

And he'd just flipped my bitch switch. "What do you mean someone like Delia? She's awesome. And if he didn't like her, why did he ask her on a date?"

"He didn't."

I replayed the events that led up to the date. Damn it. Grant was right. He'd suggested a double date and Aiden had gone along with the idea. "But Delia is great. Once he gets to know her I'm sure he'll like her."

"She's not his type." He moved his arm from my shoulders and leaned back.

Two things were becoming painfully clear. He hadn't asked me out here to kiss me, and he was saying things he knew would piss me off. I leaned in. "It's almost like you're trying to start a fight with me."

"That's ridiculous."

"Right. We were inside, having fun playing air hockey and shooting zombies. You went to the restroom. Now, we're out here, and you want to talk about someone else's date." I wrapped my arms around myself, trying to hold in body heat. "So, who said what to you in the restroom to transform the guy I was having fun with into the tool who knows I'm cold but won't put his arm around my shoulders?"

"Now I'm a tool?"

My eyes burned. "Pretty much. And you know what, this isn't a game I want to play." Blinking my eyes to keep angry tears at bay, I stood and headed into Edison's. I would find Delia and we'd call someone to come get us. Problem solved. I stalked across the patio, sneering at all the happy couples. What the hell was wrong with Grant?

Light flashed off purple hair. Delia and Aiden were making out at one of the tables near the door. A funny hollow feeling invaded my chest. Her date was going much better than mine.

I wanted to grab her and tell her about Grant's weird personality shift, but interrupting their kiss would be mortifying for all involved, so I marched into the girl's bathroom, and locked myself in a stall. Now what? Eventually Delia would come find me. When I wasn't with Grant, she'd check the restroom.

Five minutes later I realized my plan sucked. Why was I hiding in the bathroom? I wasn't the one who'd messed up. There was no telling when Delia would come up for air. Screw this. I headed back out into the game area and back over to the House of the Dead. Shooting zombies and watching their heads explode would make me feel better.

Chapter Sixteen

Grant

Zoe wasn't stupid. I had run into someone who changed my mood about the date, but it wasn't in the guy's bathroom. It was halfway across the room. A tall blonde in a tight skirt had given me a green-light smile. If I hadn't been on a date, I would've gone over and taken her number. Instead, I'd gone back to Zoe, who was smiling at me like she couldn't be happier. Then we'd come out on the patio, where—pre-tall blonde running around in my brain—I'd wanted to kiss her. Now, I didn't want Zoe to think we were a couple. And I didn't want everyone at Edison's to see us and think we were a couple. So I'd tried to start a fight.

And she'd called me on it. Now what?

I needed to find Aiden and tell him the date was over. We'd give the girls a ride home. He'd probably be happy to end the date. After all, hanging with Delia had to be awkward. Plan in mind, I headed back inside. Spotting Aiden and Delia attached at the mouth shot my plan to hell. No reason for him to end his date early.

Inside Edison's, I spotted the blonde who'd smiled at me standing with a guy who looked like he was in college. She didn't even acknowledge me. He glared at me, clenching his fists. The blonde touched his chest and said something that took his focus off me. Then he kissed her.

I'd been played.

She'd used me to make the guy she wanted jealous. I'd screwed up my date for no good reason. I needed to find Zoe and try to dig myself out of this grave.

The game room was crowded, and since Zoe was short, I had to weave through the crowd looking for her. I spotted her playing the House of the Dead game. I sidled up next to her and waited for her to notice me.

Without taking her eyes off the screen, she said, "I'm pretending that zombie is you." She pulled the trigger, brains exploded across the screen, and she smiled.

"I deserve that." More brains splattered across the screen. A group of zombies came out of nowhere. She'd be dead if she took them on by herself. I slid my Edison's card through the reader and picked up the other gun shooting the zombie closest to her.

"I had that guy," she said.

"Just trying to help."

"You shoot the guys with the chainsaws. I'll get the other ones."

"Okay." Letting someone else call the shots went against my instinct. Then again, my instincts sucked tonight.

When we'd cleared a level, and the story played, I had about thirty seconds to say something before the next horde of zombies descended. "I was a jerk."

"And?"

I pointed my gun off screen, pulling the trigger to reload.

"And I'll try not to be one again."

"That wasn't much of an apology."

The game started. We shot zombies until we ran out of lives.

"Game over," Zoe said. "Would you go get Aiden and ask him to drive me home?"

"We could play again."

"Not interested." She crossed her arms over her chest and glared at me. "I'm done with this game."

Had I really thought she wasn't the type to hold a grudge?

...

Zoe

Grant disappeared into the crowd of people. His non-apology didn't do much for the acid surging in my stomach. Neither did watching all the girls glance his way as he walked by. It was impossible not to notice him. He was gorgeous, but that didn't make up for the fact that he was an ass. What really made my head hurt was the fact that Jack had been right all along. I should have stayed away from Grant.

Delia came toward me smiling like a kid with a new toy. Then she saw the expression on my face and whacked Grant on the arm. "What did you do?"

Grant glared at Delia, but said nothing.

I didn't want to get into this in the middle of Edison's.

"Can we leave?"

"Sure." Aiden pulled the keys from his pocket. "You two wait by the door and we'll get the car."

Aiden and Grant took off for the car, and Delia gave me a questioning look. "Talk now, or later?"

"Later." Angry tears heated my eyes. If I tried to talk about the debacle my date had become I'd lose control and cry.

She pulled me into a hug. "We can make voodoo dolls if you want."

"Thanks."

The ride home was awkward. No one spoke. When we reached my house, I flung the door open. Delia called out. "Be there in a minute." I didn't know if she was kissing Aiden goodnight, or threatening Grant. Knowing her, it was probably both.

I heard the door slam, and someone jogging across the lawn. "Zoe, wait."

On my home turf, I was ready for a fight. "Wait for what, Grant? Wait for you to figure out if there's another girl you'd rather be with than me? On our date?"

He opened his mouth, but didn't say anything.

"I knew it. Some girl flirts with you on the way to the bathroom, and you decide you'd rather kiss her than me?"

"It wasn't like that."

My hands balled into fists. I wanted to punch him. If I thought I could do any damage I would have. "I've heard of guys who have trouble with the grass being greener, but never in the middle of a freaking date."

"It's not like I asked for the girl's phone number. I'm—"

I poked him in the chest. "I'm going into the house and I'm going to load one of the shotguns. If you're still here when I look out that window again, I will shoot your sorry ass and bury your body behind the barn where no one will ever find you. Do you understand?"

"We'll talk later." He backed up and headed for the car.

I stormed into the house, grabbed a shotgun off the wall and the box of shells from the china cabinet.

My grandmother came in. "Oh, dear. I take it the date didn't go well."

"No." I loaded the gun.

"While I appreciate your intent, I can't let you shoot the boy."

I cocked the gun and headed for the front door. "I told him if he wasn't gone by the time I loaded the gun, I'd shoot him."

My grandmother followed behind me. "Well, as long as you gave him fair warning."

The front door swung open, and Delia pointed at the shotgun. "Drama much? Besides they're gone."

I pushed past her and saw she was right. Tail lights weren't even visible, which meant Aiden had floored it.

My grandmother held out her hand. "I'll take care of the gun."

I squeezed the cold metal barrel of the shotgun. "I really want to shoot something."

"Tomorrow when it's light out and we won't risk killing any innocent critters, we'll go shoot cans off the fence out back."

"Fine." I passed her the gun and headed for the stairs.

"Let's go to my room."

Delia followed, and we both sat cross-legged on my bed.

"Any time you're ready," Delia said.

I grabbed a pillow and hugged it to my chest as I told her about Grant's reversal of interest. "I don't know who he met, or what she said to him. He was gone five minutes, at the most. What could the girl have said or done in that amount of time to make him lose interest?"

"That asshole." Delia squinted like she was plotting something. "He loves that car. I think we should slash his tires."

"Or put sugar in his gas tank." It was a fun fantasy, but prison orange wasn't my color.

"Sorry I wasn't there when you needed me," Delia said.

"I didn't want to ruin your date."

Delia gave a slow grin. "For a guy who drives a beige Volvo, he's pretty hot."

"How did you two end up in clinch? He doesn't seem like a guy who'd make the first move."

Delia wrinkled her nose. "It wasn't him. He was arguing with me, so I leaned over and bit him on the neck."

No way. "What did he do?"

"He froze. After I breathed in his ear, he caught on."

"Wow. Maybe I should have tried that with Grant."

"It would be a waste of time. He's one of those grass is greener kind of guys. Maybe Aiden has another friend he could introduce you to."

"That's not a bad idea." I laid the pillow flat in my lap and smoothed out the pillow case. "It's not a good idea, but it's not bad. The thing that makes me want to blow Grant's head off is the way he runs hot and cold. I'm not asking to be his girlfriend, but when a guy is on a date with me, he should be with me, not sniffing around for something better."

"Whoever it was, she wasn't better. She was a distraction. Now, it's time to plot."

...

Grant

As he drove me home, I told Aiden what happened between Zoe and me.

"Thank you for ruining what was turning out to be an interesting date." Aiden pulled up to my house and threw the car in park.

"You don't even like Delia. You said so yourself."

"I didn't say I didn't like her, I said I didn't understand her." He adjusted his glasses. "How hot could that blonde have been to make you throw me, Zoe, and Delia under the bus?"

"Unreal hot, and I didn't throw you under the bus."

"You tried to start a fight based on my date. Which means Zoe would've come to check on Delia and tell her what you said. Which means Delia and I would've ended up fighting."

"Okay. It was a dick move."

"It was and you need to find a way to make it up to Zoe, or they will seek revenge. In case you didn't notice, they both have a temper and an evil streak, which is part of what makes them so interesting. Now get out of my car."

I headed inside, avoiding the living room where my mother and father would be watching TV and not speaking to each other. Chalk their relationship up as another thing I didn't understand. Men always looked at my mother in a way that made me uncomfortable. My dad didn't seem to notice or no longer cared. I may not know what I wanted from Zoe, but I sure as hell didn't want to end up like my parents, arguing about who was higher up the social ladder.

The blonde from Edison's had been dressed like Lena and her friends. She was the type of girl my mom would approve of. Zoe, not so much. If I'd screwed things up with Zoe, what did that mean, aside from the fact that she might try to bald me or blow up my car?

I headed to my room and stared at the fish swimming circles in the saltwater tank. Around and around they went. All they wanted was food and clean water. What did I want? I knew what I didn't want. I didn't want Lena, and I didn't want a girl like her. Which left me what? Dating a girl like Zoe? Not that I'd met any other girls like her.

I pictured the blonde with her long legs and short skirt. Then I remembered her with that college guy. Next came Zoe, cheering as she shot the heads off zombies. Was that what I wanted? I didn't know, but I needed to find a way to make this right.

Sitting down at my desk, I opened my laptop and searched for all night florists who delivered. I checked the time. It was eleven thirty. Zoe and Delia would still be up.

I pulled out my American Express card and made the call.

...

Zoe

Delia and I were watching a space aliens marathon, when my cell buzzed. Who was texting me at midnight? I checked the message.

"I was an idiot. Please open your front door for the delivery guy on your porch."

"What the hell?" I showed Delia. We hopped up and looked out the picture window. There was a guy in a black tuxedo, holding a huge bouquet of roses.

"Again," I said. "What the hell?"

"There's only one way to find out." Delia unlocked the door.

The cute delivery guy in the tux said, "You must be Delia."

"Creepy." Delia started to close the door.

"Wait." The delivery guy stepped forward. "Grant told me you had purple streaks in your hair, so I'd know who was who. And I get that you think I'm a serial killer, but these are for Zoe."

I pulled the door open wider. "I'm Zoe."

He thrust the bouquet of multi colored roses at me. "There's a card, but Grant wanted me to tell you, since there wasn't a rose color that means I was a moron, he picked one of every color. Actually, he didn't say moron, but I'm not allowed to curse on the job." He gave a small bow. "If you'll excuse me, there is an idiot twenty minutes from here who told his pregnant girlfriend she looks fat."

"Oh." I cringed.

"Yeah, not sure the flowers will help him. But hey, it's an interesting job. Goodnight ladies."

Delia and I retreated to the kitchen where I put the roses in a vase. Their fragrant scent filled the air.

"What do you think?" she asked.

"I think it's funny there's a business which specializes in trying to save men after they've messed up." I pointed at a gold foil envelope hanging from a red rose. "Let's see what he has to say." I pried open the envelope and pulled out the cream colored card. In gold calligraphy, it said, "I'm sorry. And I'm not saying that just because you're plotting to blow up my car."

"There's an idea," Delia muttered.

I ignored her and kept reading. "If you want to talk, call me. If not, I understand."

Delia plucked the card from my hand and ripped it in half. "Do I need to confiscate your cell phone?"

"No. I'm not calling him tonight. He doesn't get off that easy." I touched the velvet soft petals of a yellow rose. "But he did have to find an all-night florist and I'm sure it wasn't cheap."

"He gets points for trying, but he isn't forgiven. Agreed?"

"Agreed."

...

Over breakfast my grandmother listened to the story about the delivery service and laughed. "I bet a woman started the business." She sniffed the bouquet. "Nothing smells like fresh roses."

Jack sat at the kitchen table with his ear buds in, wolfing down a plate of toaster waffles and pretending he couldn't hear what we were saying. This was his standard approach to being anywhere near Delia. They had a hate-hate relationship.

"Are you going to call him?" my grandma asked.

"Not today."

"Good. It doesn't matter how cute a boy is, or how much you like him, he should never treat you like you're second rate."

Delia squirted syrup on her waffles. "I still think we should do something to his car."

"I'll pretend I didn't hear that," Grandma said. "Now who's up for target practice behind the barn?"

Chapter Seventeen

Zoe

Jack said nothing to me as we drove to school. Or if he did, I didn't hear him, because I had ear buds in, listening to music on my phone. At least I was attempting to listen to music. In my head, I ran through every scenario I could think of about how Grant would react when he saw me today. Would he come find me and apologize? Would he ignore me? The possibilities were agonizing and endless.

One thing I knew for sure, I would not look for him. Delia and I planned to meet at our usual spot and if Grant wanted to try apologizing again, he could come find me. And if he didn't, I'd move on.

Once I was standing with Delia in our usual spot, I drank my coffee and focused on not scanning the crowd for dark wavy hair and ice blue eyes. The clock tower on the quad told me Grant had fifteen minutes to make an appearance.

Where the heck was he?

"Don't worry, he'll be here," Delia said.

"How do you know?"

"He's a guy. Once you tell him he can't have something, he's going to want it more."

I didn't love her logic. But I couldn't argue against it. The minutes ticked by. With every second that passed I told myself I was better off without him. I deserved someone who would put me first, not someone on a constant look out for his next date. "Let's go to class."

Delia checked her cell. "He still has five minutes."

"I'm done waiting."

Seated in first hour, I could feel Lena watching me, waiting to pounce at the first sign of weakness. Eyes on the board, I ignored her and did my best to focus on the lecture. When it came time to pass papers back, I took a deep breath and plastered a relaxed expression on my face.

"Heard your date didn't go too well." Lena spoke in a voice which had ha-ha laced through it.

Someone from Edison's must have gossiped about the fight Grant and I had on the patio. Good to know the rumor mill was alive and well. "It didn't. He apologized and sent flowers, but I'm still ticked off."

Her eyes narrowed. "You're lying."

"Believe what you want." I turned back around reveling in my small victory.

After class, as Delia and I walked down the hall, I forced myself not to scan for Grant.

"Zoe." I recognized the male voice, but it wasn't the one I wanted to hear.

Delia and I turned around.

"Hi." Aiden smiled at Delia and then his gaze settled on me. "Grant wanted me to tell you he's not at school today, because his grandfather had a heart attack."

Well, crap. "Is his grandpa okay?"

"They're putting a stent in today. Supposedly it's not a big deal. His grandfather has to lay off cigars and greasy food."

"That's not so bad."

"He should be fine." Aiden glanced at Delia and then looked away. "So uhm...see you later."

...

I missed Grant in Foods class, but whipped up a batch of Rice Krispies treats with chocolate and butterscotch chips that were awesome. No matter how ticked off I was, I couldn't help worrying about him. I knew what it was like to have someone you loved end up in the hospital.

Should I call and ask how he was doing? No. He had friends to talk to. He didn't need my shoulder to lean on.

After school I'd barely made it through my front door when Grant texted me. "Can we talk?"

Did I really want to get into this? Then again, it wasn't fair to kick a guy when he was down. I texted back. "Call me in five minutes." And headed for my bedroom.

The phone rang exactly five minutes later. "Zoe?"

"Hi. How's your grandpa?"

"He's doing better."

"Good."

I heard a yawn through the phone. "Sorry. I didn't get much sleep last night."

"Understandable."

"Listen, I wanted to apologize again. I was an idiot."

"You were a jerk."

"I know. Let me make it up to you. I need to get out of the house. Why don't I come get you? We could talk over dinner."

My heart rate kicked up a notch. "I'm not sure that's a good idea."

He sighed. "I deserve that, but I need to talk to someone who isn't going to expect me to act like everything is all right."

Dang it. "Okay, but this isn't a date."

"Thanks. See you in half an hour."

He hung up. I changed into my after school outfit of comfortable jeans and a sweatshirt. It's not like I was trying to impress him and I sort of wanted him to realize that. Then I sat outside on the porch swing crocheting a scarf, and waited for Grant.

When he pulled into the driveway in his shiny black sports car, I rolled up the twelve inches of gray scarf I'd made so far, shoved the crochet needle into the skein, and took it with me to his car.

The first thing I noticed about Grant was the dark circles under his eyes. "You look like hell."

"Gee, thanks."

I laughed. "Sorry. You wanted someone who would tell you the truth."

"You're right." He rubbed at his eyes and yawned. "You'd think they'd make hospital waiting rooms with cots in them instead of those god-awful plastic chairs."

I'd spent a few nights in those chairs. "I know, and they keep those rooms at ice box temperatures and the TV's only show depressing news stories."

"Sounds like you spent some time in the hospital, too."

"Too much." My chest ached at the memories. "My dad and my grandpa were in an accident together. They both held on for a little while before—" and I couldn't get any more out without crying.

"I'm sorry." Grant leaned over and wrapped his arms around me.

He smelled like dryer sheets and soap. I held onto him for a minute, enjoying the warmth until I wrangled my tear ducts under control, and then pulled back. "I'm supposed to be taking care of you right now. Let's talk about something else."

My stomach growled loud enough for Grant to hear.

"Right. Food." He put the car into drive, did a three point turn and headed back down the road. "Where do you want to go?"

"The closest place is Betty's Burgers. I'm okay with that if you are."

We made safe small talk until we were seated in Betty's. Grant ordered a double bacon cheeseburger and fries. I ordered a burger and fries.

"Did I miss anything exciting at school today?" he asked.

"Only the best Rice Krispie Treats ever."

He made a yuck face. "I've never liked those."

"Did you ever have any with chocolate and butterscotch chips?"

"No."

"Don't knock it till you try it."

Our food came. We ate and talked until Grant's eyes started to drift shut.

"We should probably go before you fall asleep."

"I drank a soda." He yawned. "I can't believe I'm this tired."

"Are you okay to drive?"

"I think so."

I held my hand out. "Give me the keys."

"Not a chance."

"You'd rather die in a fiery car crash than let me drive your car?"

He pretended to think about it. "Yes."

"You're an idiot." Saying that out loud brought me a certain amount of joy. "I'm capable of driving your car. Nothing will happen to it, and no one will die. It's a win-win situation."

"No. It's a stupid idea. If you drive me home how will you get back to your house?"

Hmmm. Good question. "I would suggest that I drive your car back to my house and then come pick you up tomorrow for school, but I'm pretty sure that idea would give you a seizure, so how about I'll call Delia or my grandma to come get me."

"I'm fine." He reached for the check the waitress had dropped on our table and knocked his drink over in the process.

"Those reflexes are as sharp as ever, all right." I mopped up the soda with my napkin.

"Smart ass."

He ordered a refill on his soda to go, we paid the bill, and despite my protests, he climbed behind the wheel.

Muttering under my breath, I put on my seatbelt.

Getting the metal tab into the slot was harder than it should be, because I'd twisted the strap around somehow. Finally, it clicked, and I looked up to see Grant's face an inch from mine.

"Uhm, hi there."

He leaned forward, like he was going to kiss me.

I jerked backward.

"What? Do I have bad breath?" he asked.

"No. I appreciate the flowers and the apology, but you still tried to ditch me on our date."

He stared up at the ceiling. "I've apologized several times."

"True, but I need to know when we're together you're not scanning the room for a better option."

"It's not like there's anyone else in the car."

"Wow. That makes me feel so much better. Since I'm your only choice at the moment, I guess I don't have anything to worry about."

He rubbed his eyes. "That's not what I meant. I didn't get shit for sleep last night."

"And?" Time for him to step up and tell me he wanted to be with me.

"And I never thought I'd be into a girl who shoots zombies. And this is all weird. And when my life went to hell, you were the first person I wanted to talk to and that has to mean something. And would you just shut up and kiss me now?"

I'd like to, but I wasn't sure I could trust him. "If I kiss you, what does it mean?"

"It means you're giving me another chance. I swear I won't mess up like that again." He leaned in, and this time, I met him halfway.

What can I say? I wanted to believe him. Hopefully I wouldn't regret this. He wrapped his arms around me and pulled me as close as the seat belt allowed. It felt right.

Kaboom!

Grant could kiss, but I figured whatever rattled the car, came from someplace else. I opened my eyes. Lightning arced across the sky. Rain pelted the car. It sounded like we were under attack by a BB gun militia.

"What the heck?" This better not be a comment on my relationship with Grant from a higher power.

"Maybe it's fate." Grant pushed the button on my seatbelt, sending the buckle flying back over my shoulder. He slid his hand behind my lower back and pulled me as close as the gear shift allowed. I wrapped my arms around his neck and threw myself into the kiss. His right hand slid under my sweatshirt resting against the small of my back.

Warmth radiated from his touch.

Kaboom.

I flinched, smacking my teeth against his. "Ow." I pulled back. The metallic taste of blood hit my taste buds. "Sorry." Who was the biggest dork in the world? Me. Hands down. I forced a laugh.

He rubbed his lip, but he didn't look angry. "You all right?"

"Terminally embarrassed, but otherwise fine." I grimaced at the taste in my mouth. "Can I have a drink of your soda?"

"Sure"

I took a few sips and the metallic taste went away. It must be Grant's lip that was bleeding. Great, I actually wanted to kiss him now, and I'd rendered him incapable.

I offered him the soda. He took a sip and swished it around his mouth.

The rain drops seemed to slow. Grant leaned forward and peered out the window. "Maybe the worst of it's over."

Pretending I was interested in watching water fall from the sky, I leaned forward. The rain did seem to be slowing down.

"Think we should try driving now?" he asked.

"Are you sure you're all right to drive?"

"I'm good." He drove back to my house without incident and parked in the driveway.

"Call me to let me know you made it home safe, okay?" He just stared at me for a moment.

"What?"

"No one besides my grandfather has ever said that to me." He leaned in and gave me a soft kiss. "Good night."

I climbed out of the car and went into the house, watching out the window as his tail lights faded into the distance.

...

Grant

Aiden was sitting with Zoe and Delia Wednesday afternoon when I entered the cafeteria. Funny how that seemed normal now. Since Monday, I'd fallen into an easy routine of meeting Zoe before school, eating with her at lunch, and walking her out to the parking lot after school. Kissing her goodbye while her brother sat in the car was a bonus.

Zoe spotted me and her face lit up like I was the best thing she'd ever seen. I'll admit it. I liked it. With Zoe, there was no pretense, no games. I grabbed three slices of pizza and joined her at the table.

"I was about to send out a search party." She snatched a piece of pepperoni off my plate.

"I was stuck playing ambassador to a freshman who moved in."

"What's he like?" Aiden asked.

"She is annoying." Okay. She hadn't been that bad, but I didn't want Zoe thinking I had any ulterior motives.

"A new girl?" Zoe said. "I wonder if she'll dethrone the freshman princess."

"What does that mean?"

"Please. The only thing worse than a bunch of guys jockeying for the alpha male position is the socialites climbing on top of each other to prove who wears the tiara."

"And where do you fit in this royal scheme?" I asked.

"I am creator of my own reality," Zoe said. "So, I am queen of the universe."

"Grant?" A girl said from behind me.

My shoulder muscles tensed. I knew that voice. Turning to face my ex, I said, "What do you want, Lena?"

"The Fall dance is coming up, I need to know how you want to handle the situation."

Shit. I'd forgotten.

"What's she talking about?" Zoe asked.

This was going to be ugly. "You had to bring this up in the cafeteria where we'd have the biggest audience, didn't you?"

Lena batted her eyes at me. "It's more fun this way."

I turned to Zoe. "This is going to sound worse than it is. Last year, Lena and I were nominated the Fall Dance Queen and King. So this year—"

"He's my date," Lena said loud enough for everyone to hear.

I expected Zoe to rip my head off, or throw down with Lena. She just laughed.

"What's she talking about?"

"Traditionally," I said, "we're supposed to pass the crown on to another couple."

"You don't need to be her date to do that," Zoe said. "We'll go together. When it's time to pass on the absurd head gear, go on stage or wherever it is you go to perform these archaic rituals, and pass on the silly things."

"That's not how it works," Lena said.

"That's how it's going to work this year," Zoe said. "Right, Grant?"

"Yes." It was as good a solution as any I could come up with.

"Fine." Lena stomped back to her table of minions.

"That was pitiful," Zoe said.

I laughed.

"The dance is this Saturday, isn't it?" Delia asked, glancing at Aiden.

He pretended to find his sandwich fascinating. "I wouldn't know. I don't attend dances."

Chapter Eighteen

Zoe

Apparently Aiden couldn't take a hint.

"You never go to dances?" Delia asked.

"No," Aiden said. "They're loud and crowded."

"That's just sad." Delia stood. "Zoe, want to get out of here?"

"Sure." I grabbed my backpack and we headed for the door. Outside the cafeteria, she chose a bench and plopped down.

"I'm beginning to think Aiden is a lost cause." She dug into her backpack and pulled out a handful of Hershey's kisses, unwrapped one and ate it while she unwrapped another.

"You guys are polar opposites. He's so shy. You need a guy who is more outgoing."

"You're probably right. His loss."

Delia and I went our separate ways after lunch. In Foods class, I tried to pry information from Grant about his pain in the butt friend.

"Zoe, I don't know what you want me to say. Aiden does what he wants. If Delia wants to go the dance, she'll have to go with someone else, because Aiden isn't going."

"Couldn't you talk him into going?"

"No."

Normally, Grant walking me to my car and kissing me goodbye in front of my brother was one of my favorite parts of the day. But today, I was feeling less than romantic. "Aiden didn't tell you anything?"

Grant pointed at me. "Female." Then he pointed at himself. "Male. We don't talk about everything like you do."

Honk. Honk.

My idiot brother laid on the horn.

"Like that's going to make me move faster." I reached up and wrapped my arms around Grant's neck. He kissed me, backing me up against the car. The cold metal at my back contrasted with the heat of his body pressed against mine.

Honk. Honk. Honk.

"I hate your brother." Grant kissed me one last time. "See you tomorrow."

After dinner, I lay on my bed staring up at the spider web of cracks in the plaster of my ceiling, talking to Delia about the cake we planned to bake for the auction. We'd been on the phone so long my ear was hot.

"I found these cupcakes on Pinterest," she said. "They're normal cupcakes, but there's what looks like a book on top of each one."

"Like a paper book?" I asked.

"No. It looks like clay."

"That would be tasty." I laughed, and thought for a minute. "I bet it's fondant or marzipan."

"I think you just made those words up."

"Fondant is really stiff icing," I explained." And marzipan is almond paste."

Beep.

"Someone is trying to call through." I checked caller ID, but all it said was private caller. "I don't recognize the number. Hold on."

I clicked over. "Hello?"

"May I speak to Monica?" a man asked.

It took a moment for me to realize he meant my grandmother. "Sure."

Clicking back over, I told Delia I'd talk to her tomorrow and went in search of my grandma. She sat on the couch reading a spy novel. "Phone for you."

She closed her book. "Who is it?"

I held the phone out to her. "I don't know." My grandmother crossed her arms and waited.

"Fine." I clicked on the phone. "I forgot to ask who this was, and my grandmother doesn't like surprises." She swatted at me with her book.

He laughed. It was a warm sound. "Tell her at our age she should enjoy the mystery."

I shoved the phone at my grandma, repeating his message.

She put the phone to her ear. "All right, mystery man. You have five seconds to dazzle me before I hang up." Her cheeks colored. "Everett, it's been a long time."

Wait a minute. Everett, as in Everett Evertide? Grant's grandpa? Why was he calling my grandma? And why was my grandma blushing?

I dashed upstairs and checked my cell. Fifteen percent charged. That would have to do. Grant answered on the fifth ring.

"Zoe?"

"What took you so long?"

"Hold on. I just got out of the shower."

A naked Grant. My insides shimmied around in an exciting kind of way, and my face colored. Just like my grandma's. Holy crap. Was my grandma thinking about Grant's grandpa naked? Now my insides shimmied in a not so good way.

"I'm back," Grant said. "What's up?"

"Why—" My voice cracked. I cleared my throat and tried again. "Why is your grandfather calling my grandma?"

"How would I know...oh shit. Earlier tonight, he was talking about how the heart attack made him realize he needed to start living again."

"Ick. I mean good for him, but why can't he hit on someone else's grandma?"

"Maybe it's not what we think. Maybe they're old friends."

Laughter drifted up from downstairs. Suspicion confirmed. "I don't think that's it."

"Maybe I should remind him about the shotguns," Grant said, not in a joking voice.

"Please, if she knows he had a heart attack, she won't threaten to shoot him unless he deserves it."

...

Delia called while I was blow drying my hair the next morning. "I'm coming to pick you up. I need your opinion on something."

Before I could say okay, she hung up. I shouted to Jack that I wouldn't be riding with him, finished my hair, and added some eyeliner and lip gloss. What did Delia want my opinion about? Her plan to find a new guy? Her plot to make Aiden like dances? The options were wide open, which made the day a little more exciting.

When she walked in the kitchen, I figured out she was talking about her new look.

"Holy shit," Jack said from the kitchen table where he sat eating his pop tart.

She ignored him and focused on me. "Well?"

Her hair was shot through with crimson streaks. Her lips and nails were glossy red. Her eyes, accented by smoky eyeliner and thick lashes made her look like some sort of Goth Snow White.

"You look awesome." I hugged her.

"Thank you. I was afraid it might be too much."

I snorted. "I can't believe you managed to say that with a straight face."

She laughed. "You're right. I figured if I planned to look for a new guy, I should have a new look."

"At least one of you is smart enough to avoid assholes," my brother commented.

"It's hard to avoid them when you live with one," I shot back.

...

In first hour, Lena gave Delia the once over and muttered something rude under her breath. I couldn't quite make it out, but I knew it was mean. Delia must have figured out the same thing.

"You're jealous because you couldn't pull this off," Delia said loud enough for other people to hear.

"Please, gothic hick isn't a look I aspire to."

Delia's eyes narrowed. "Maybe you should branch out, since you have snotty rich bitch down to a science." Students around us sucked in their breath.

Mr. Fletcher entered the room, and took note of the stare down. "Ladies, if you could declare a stalemate for now, I'd like to start class. If not, I can assign detention now to save time later."

"Not necessary," Delia said. "I'm done with her."

Chapter Nineteen

Zoe

At lunch, Aiden was conspicuously absent from our table. Since Delia didn't comment, I wasn't going to mention it. Grant squirted ketchup on his fries in the spider web pattern he favored.

"Why do you do that?" I asked.

"Do what?"

"Why do you play Spiderman with your ketchup?" I pointed at the pattern he'd made. "Most people put it all in one spot." I pointed at my plate where I'd squirted three packets next to my fries in the normal fashion.

He shrugged. "I don't know. I guess it's the way my grandpa showed me how to do it."

Interesting. Maybe I'd ask my grandma if she remembered Everett doing the same thing. How weird to compare dating notes with my grandma.

"Did you look at the picture of the cupcakes I sent you from Pinterest?" Delia asked.

"Yes." I grabbed my phone and pulled up the link. "It's fondant. I think we could do it. We should practice making the books without the cupcakes since that's the tricky part."

"Okay. Tonight it's Operation Fondant at your house."

Later that night, we surveyed the mess that was my kitchen counter.

"Fondant is evil." I glared at the rectangular cracked piece of icing that looked nothing like a book.

"Agreed." Delia pushed her fondant sculpture away. It looked better than mine, but not by much. "Now what?"

I rolled my shoulders trying to make the tension go away. "It's still nice out. Let's walk to the pond."

We cleaned up, and then headed down the dirt path that ran alongside my house to the pond. My dad had planned to put in a gravel road so we wouldn't have to deal with mud, but he didn't get around to it. A twinge of sadness made me catch my breath. The cool breeze, or maybe it was my melancholy thoughts, raised goose bumps on my arms.

Delia wrapped her arms around her chest. "We should have grabbed jackets."

"It feels good. I like when the temperature drops. It means winter is on its way."

"Not all of us enjoy being snowed in," Delia said.

"It's nature's way of telling us to slow down and enjoy the moment. As long as you have food and water, you're good. You can't leave your house, so you don't have to hurry to get anywhere. It's like a mini-vacation."

"That's one way to look at it."

When we reached the pond, I sat on the grass while Delia collected stones from the edge of the man-made pond. My dad had dredged the area, lined it with sand, and then added landscaping rock all around the edge. He'd chosen a blend of smooth and rough stones because if all the rocks were smooth, you'd never feel the joy of finding the perfect skipping stone.

Thinking about him made my chest ache.

Delia drew her arm back and whizzed a rock across the top of the water. It skipped three times before sinking.

"Nice," I commented.

"Your turn." Delia held a rock out to me.

"You know how this will turn out." I stood and took the rock, performed the exact same arm maneuver Delia had, and watched as my rock hit the water and sunk. "See, I still suck at this."

"True." Delia laughed and flung another stone, which skipped across the water, shooting up a small spray three times before sinking. "We both suck at making fondant icing. What are we going to do?"

"Maybe we give up on the book idea and pick something else," I said. "Go in a new decorating direction."

"Maybe we should just make fancy cupcakes that someone might want to take home and set out for a party."

"That would be easier, and someone would be likelier to bid on those because they'd be easier to share," I said. "We can Google pictures of cupcakes from those high end cupcake specialty stores for inspiration."

Delia skipped another stone across the pond. "I like it."

"Good." I liked having a new plan. "Operation Fancy Cupcakes is a go."

Chapter Twenty

Grant

Aiden texted Friday at seven a.m. and asked if I could give him a ride to school. He didn't say why, and I didn't have time to ask questions if I wanted to make it to school on time. He waited for me at the edge of his driveway.

"What's up?" I asked as he climbed in.

"My dad backed into my car last night, which is somehow my fault even though I parked where I always park." Aiden adjusted his glasses, pushing them farther up on the bridge of his nose. "I pointed out that his logic was faulty."

"I'm sure that made the situation better."

"Yeah, it was a brilliant move on my part."

"Speaking of brilliant moves, what's going on with you and Delia?"

"Nothing."

"I thought you liked her."

He shrugged.

"Maybe you should—"

"Stop. I don't need your help. It's not like you are qualified to give dating advice."

"I'm doing better than you are."

"Really? You didn't want a girlfriend, but that's exactly what you have."

"I do not. Zoe and I are dating. That's it."

"So you wouldn't mind if I asked her whether or not she thinks she's your girlfriend?"

"Try it, and I'll punch you in the throat."

"Exactly."

When we made it to school, Zoe wasn't where she usually stood in quad. That was weird. Where was she?

"Looking for your girlfriend?" Aiden asked.

"Shut up." I punched him on the arm and then I went back to scanning the crowd for Zoe. She stood near the entrance to the building with Delia and they weren't alone. I didn't care that Delia was talking to some guy, but another guy was talking to Zoe and he was standing a little too close. I headed for my not-girlfriend. The guy moved closer to Zoe and touched her on the arm.

Now I wanted to punch him in the throat.

To Zoe's credit, she backed away from the interloper.

When she saw me she waved.

"Good morning." Zoe came toward me.

"Morning." Instead of putting my arm around her shoulder like I normally did, I kissed her. She seemed startled at first. Once she caught on, she threw her arms around my neck and threaded her fingers through my hair.

"Mr. Evertide."

I pretended not to hear whoever was lecturing me. Zoe laughed against my mouth and stepped back.

Turning to find Ms. Ida smiling at me was a surprise. "I knew you two would make a good team. However, you know the school policy. I'm afraid you'll both have to report to the principal's office after school."

I nodded, not caring about detention. The way Zoe was still clinging to me showed she didn't care either.

"I wonder if the school has a double indemnity clause." She wiggled her eyebrows. "We already have detention."

So I kissed her again. This time, the tone signaling five minutes until first hour broke us apart. I walked Zoe to her class, and then went to mine. Happy with the message I'd sent for other guys to stay away from my girl—oh hell. I'd been about to think of her as my girlfriend. It was Aiden's fault for putting that idea into my head.

...

Zoe

By the end of the day, I was torn between being happy for myself that Grant was taking me to the dance, and being sad for Delia because she wasn't going.

Delia met up with me outside the principal's office. "I can help you get ready for the dance tomorrow, if you want."

Crap. How was I supposed to handle this? "We could get ready together, and you could go with us. I'm sure Grant wouldn't mind."

"Yeah, right." She tucked a strand of crimson hair behind her ear. "Don't worry about it. It's not a big deal. I'll play with your hair and makeup, and then

I'll swing by Betty's and pick up a I didn't want to go to the stupid dance anyway chocolate chip pecan pie on my way home."

"I bet a pie with that name would sell really well. We'll create one and sell it in our bakery boutique along with Boys are idiots cupcakes."

Delia laughed. "We may have just stumbled on marketing gold."

Grant showed up. If the frown on his face was any indication, he was less than happy.

"Call me," Delia said as she left.

"What's with the face?" I asked Grant. Would I be eating pie with Delia rather than going to the dance tomorrow? Because that would suck.

"Remember the last time we had detention and Principal Stephens didn't have time to call our parents?"

Crap. I'd totally forgotten. "He's definitely going to call our parents this time."

"The good news is, my mom should be shopping with friends, and my dad won't be home to answer the phone. What about you?"

"My mom was planning to hit the grocery store after work tonight, which means he'll probably reach my grandma. That won't be so bad."

He grabbed my hand and led me into the office.

"You two again." The secretary dug the dead chicken timer out of the drawer. "Have a seat. Principal Stephens will call you into the office once your parents arrive."

Grant and I sat at the table, checking the door every time someone walked in. The third time the door opened, my grandmother walked in, smiling. Spotting me, she scowled like a villain from a cartoon, which made me laugh.

"Quiet," the secretary snapped.

It took a great amount of self control not to roll my eyes. After my grandmother signed in, she sat in a chair outside the principal's office, pulled out a steel blue scarf she was crocheting, and went to work.

The door opened, and Grant frowned. A petite brunette walked in, looking like she was ready to sue the entire school into the dust. She had to be his mother. The way she carried herself reminded me of Lena. I would so have to torture Grant about that later.

His mom didn't acknowledge the secretary or bother signing in. She marched straight back toward the principal's office.

"Ma'am, you have to sign in," the secretary said in a much nicer tone than she'd used with us.

"Do you know who I am?" Grant's mom said, in a voice that carried through the office.

Grant ducked his head, like he was embarrassed of his mom's behavior.

"If you signed in, she'd know who you were," my grandmother said in a conversational tone.

Grant's mom zeroed in on my grandma. She examined her from head to toe. Apparently my grandmother's jeans and thermal pink camo shirt didn't pass inspection, because she sneered and then said, "Who are you?"

Pretending not to notice what a bitch Grant's mom was being, my grandmother set down the scarf she was working on and held out her hand. "I'm Monica Cain. And you are?"

The principal's door opened, and the man himself stepped outside. "Sorry to keep you waiting, ladies. Please come in."

Would we have to go in there with them?

"Zoe, Grant, in here. Now."

That answered that question. I pushed my chair back and sighed.

Grant stood. He opened his mouth to say something and then stopped.

"Your mom is going to hate me, isn't she?"

He cringed and then turned and headed for the open door where the principal waited, irritation clear on his face.

...

It was awkward with all five of us shoved in Principal Stephen's office. The adults sat in the chairs, while Grant and I stood wedged in on the side of his desk so all three of them could glare at us. Although my grandma wasn't really glaring. Grant's mom could've stared down an axe murderer.

"I'm sorry to disturb you ladies, but this is the third time Grant and Zoe have been cited for PDA's."

"I'm sorry," my grandmother said. "I'm not sure what you mean."

I was sure she knew what he meant, and she was just messing with the man. I ducked my head like I was embarrassed, but I was trying not to smile.

"They've been caught kissing on school grounds." Principal Stephens sat straighter in his chair and adjusted his tie.

Grant's mom gave me the once over. "You think this is a girl worth getting in trouble over? If it was someone like Lena, I could understand, but her...it's ridiculous."

My face heated, and I wanted to slap the smug expression off her face.

Grant's arm went around my waist. "Mother, I—"

"Excuse me, Grant," my grandma said, in her I'm about to load the shotgun voice. "What do you mean my granddaughter isn't worth getting in trouble over? She's smart, she's beautiful."

Grant's mom snorted. "Cute maybe, but not beautiful."

"Ladies, if we could return to the problem at hand?" Principal Stephens tugged at his tie.

"The problem at hand is this woman seems to think she can insult my granddaughter without retaliation. And that isn't true." My grandmother shook her head. "Everett told me you were a pill. I thought he was being mean, but now I see he was being generous."

"Everett? My father-in-law? Why were you speaking to him?"

"We're dating, dear. He invited me to dinner at your house this Sunday."

"Trying to pad your retirement account?" Grant's mom asked.

"It's a wonder how so much bitchiness can be contained in such a small woman," my grandmother shot back.

I laughed. Grant's face turned red. And Principal Stephens looked like he wanted to crawl under his desk.

Grant's mom stood, pointing her finger at my grandma. "I want her thrown off school grounds. And I want her granddaughter kicked out of Wilton."

"Mrs. Evertide, I'm sure that's not necessary." Principal Stephens stood and gestured that Grant and I should move toward the door. "I'm sure Zoe and Grant understand the error of their ways."

"I said, I want that girl kicked out of Wilton. She's a bad influence on my son."

"No she's not," Grant said.

"Sorry to cut this meeting short, ladies, but I have an appointment this evening." He grabbed his coat. "Zoe, get the door please."

Sure. Why not? I opened the door, and Principal Stephens was out of his office like a shot. Smart man.

Grant pushed me out the door in front of him. "We're grabbing dinner somewhere, Mother. I'll see you later."

I checked over my shoulder and saw my grandma pick up her purse and walk past Grant's mom, like she couldn't hear the tirade of bitchiness pouring from her mouth.

"Don't make eye contact." Grant took my hand and pulled me out the door, running down the hall.

By the time we made it to his car, we were both laughing.

He floored it out of the parking lot and pulled over onto a side street before we reached the highway.

"Where are we going?"

"We are off school grounds." He undid his seatbelt and pushed the button to release mine.

"What—"

And then he kissed me. The gearshift was digging into my ribs, and the seatbelt was hung up on my right arm, but none of that mattered. Grant's mouth moved against mine, and his hands slid up the back of my shirt, and my skin tingled wherever he touched. And now the gear shift was annoying me, because I wanted to be closer.

When Grant pulled away, we were both winded. He leaned his forehead against mine. "I should have bought an automatic transmission."

"Yes, you should have."

His smile dimmed. "Sorry about my mom."

I cringed, remembering his mom's words. "She really doesn't like me."

"Her opinion doesn't count." He brushed his lips across mine. "I like you. And I'm keeping you."

Wait. Did that mean what I thought it meant? It sounded like he was saying I was his girlfriend. Was he saying that? Or was I hearing what I wanted to hear? Better not to ask.

Time to play it cool. "I guess it's a good thing I like you, too."

"Well, that was a given." He smiled, daring me to argue the point.

I rolled my eyes. "It's your humble streak that keeps me hooked."

"That and my baking skills." His stomach growled. "Food. We need food."

Fifteen minutes later, we were at a Chinese restaurant I'd never been to, in one of the nicer areas downtown. It was twenty minutes from school, which meant it would take him fifty minutes to drive me home and about the same amount of time for him to get home. Had he put that together yet?

Everyone else in the restaurant wore suits or dresses. I tugged at my white blouse, trying to straighten out some of the wrinkles.

"What are you doing?" Grant asked.

I dropped my hands. "I feel underdressed."

"You're fine." He flipped his menu over. "Do you know what you want?"

Problem number two, my experience with Chinese food ran from fried rice to beef and broccoli. Neither of those dishes were on the menu.

"What are you having?" Maybe I could copy something close to his order.

"I like the Mu Shoo Chicken."

And I had no idea what that was. Time to confess. "I usually order chicken fried rice, but I don't see it on here."

"You'd probably like this." He pointed at something I couldn't pronounce if I tried.

"Sure. That looks good." The waitress approached our table wearing a chic emerald silk dress which skimmed her body. Great. Even the waitress was dressed better than I was. "Will you order for me while I go wash my hands?"

I made my escape and headed for the restrooms. What was wrong with me? A quick check in the mirror showed my hair and makeup were doing their standard thing. It must be Grant's mom inside my head, telling me I wasn't good enough. I needed to find a way to evict that woman from my subconscious. Grant liked me and that's what mattered.

I plastered on a smile and marched back out to our table, only to find Grant had replaced me. Sitting next to him, were twin, tan, and more than likely tall, blondes. I hated them on sight. Who were these obnoxiously perfect girls and why were they sitting with my boyfriend, I mean my date?

Grant smiled up at me, so I smiled back, pretending I wasn't five seconds from stabbing him in the heart with a chopstick.

"Zoe, this is Angeline and Georgette Turner. They graduated from Wilton a few years ago."

I waited for him to tell them I was his girlfriend, or his date. Anything to indicate my status as more than a friend.

He didn't say any of those things, so I took the high road. "Nice to meet you." Now get the hell out of my chair.

"How do you know Grant?" Twin One asked.

Opportunity number two for Grant to acknowledge me in some manner. Nothing. Nada. Zip. "We're dating."

"Oh." Twin number two said.

"We haven't seen Grant since we summered in San Francisco with him last year." Twin number one said.

"Do you have a condo in San Francisco?" Twin number two asked.

They knew the answer to the question before they asked it. I wasn't playing their game. "No. I live here year round."

"That must be boring." Twin number one wrinkled her nose.

Twin number two nodded in agreement.

And I was done. "It's not. Now, unless you'd like me to sit on your lap, I suggest you remove yourself from my chair."

The waitress arrived with our food. She set Grant's plate in front of him, and then glanced at me. "Where are you sitting?"

"Good question. Grant, where am I sitting?"

He gave a tight smile. "Angeline, Georgette, it was nice seeing you. We'll catch up some other time."

The blondes made a show of acting offended. If they didn't vacate the area immediately, I was going to give them a much better reason to be offended.

Once they were gone, I reclaimed my seat and dug into my food.

"What was that about?" Grant asked.

"You'll have to be more specific." I shoveled a forkful of rice and chicken into my mouth. With the way this was going, it might be a good idea to eat fast.

"Why were you rude to my friends?"

Seriously? "They were rude to me first."

"No they weren't. Angeline asked you a question."

Was he deaf and blind? "No. She asked a question she knew the answer to, like I was supposed to be ashamed of not having a condo somewhere, and she called my life boring."

"Well, they travel year round. To them living in one place would be boring."

A chopstick to the heart was happening in ten seconds if he didn't take my side. "It's rude to call someone's life boring. And why do you care so much about their feelings and so little about mine?"

"Why are you overreacting? They were making small talk."

I needed to make him understand. "If I said, oh, you only have one car? How boring. I have a different car for every day of the week. How would you take that?"

He poured soy sauce on his food and took a bite. After an agonizing amount of time, he said. "I guess I can see your point. But I don't think they meant it that way."

A swing and a miss. "You do realize they were being bitchy to me because one of them likes you." God forbid it was both of them. Competing with one would be bad enough.

He seemed surprised by this fact. "Really?"

"You don't have to sound so happy about it."

"Sorry. It's just that I had a crush on Angeline when I was a freshman and she was a junior. She was way out of my league."

"And now she's not." I sat back and crossed my arms over my chest. "Would you like to run over to her table and get her number before we leave?" And that sounded much bitchier out loud than it had in my head.

Grant took a deep breath, like he was trying not to say something.

I knew what it was. He was going to tell me not to be jealous, because we weren't dating exclusively. And I didn't want to hear him say it.

"Zoe, we—"

"Please don't finish that sentence. Not here. We can talk on the car ride back to my house." Which now seemed like it would be fifty minutes of hell.

We finished our meal in silence, and walked to the car in silence, and drove for the first ten minutes in silence, and then I couldn't take it anymore.

"Go ahead and finish what you started to say." Heart in my throat, I held my breath and waited.

Chapter Twenty-One

Grant

"What do you want me to say?" I didn't hide the irritation in my voice.

She sniffled. Oh hell. Was she crying? This is exactly what I didn't want. "Zoe, talk to me."

"Why didn't you tell the twins we were dating?"

"We were sitting together eating dinner. I assumed they'd realize we were dating."

"And that's what we're doing? Dating?"

What was she getting at? "What else would you call it?"

"I don't know. You keep sending me mixed signals. One minute you tell me you like me and you're keeping me. Then you're smiling about some other girl liking you."

"Angeline is a former crush. I'm flattered that she'd like me now, when she wouldn't give me the time of day before. I don't understand why you're getting bent out of shape about this."

"If we went to Betty's for burgers, and a cute guy came over to our table and flirted with me, and you found out he's a guy I used to like, and I didn't tell him we were dating, would you be a happy camper?"

She had a point...then again, I could date who I wanted. I checked the next exit number. We had thirty more minutes together in the car. So this probably wasn't the best time to bring up our non-exclusive dating status.

"I should have said we were dating. Next time, I'll explain the situation if that will make you feel better."

"I'd feel better if you hadn't used the implied idiot tone when you said that."

Well this was going to be a fun ride. I gripped the steering wheel tighter. "Zoe. We talked about this."

"And here it comes."

Why did all girls have to be like this? "It's not like I'm springing something on you. We said we weren't dating exclusively."

"That was before you told me that you liked me and you were keeping me. When you said that, I thought you meant something that you obviously didn't."

Well, shit. "I meant what I said. I like you and I don't care who doesn't like you. That doesn't mean I'm ready to date anyone exclusively."

"Right. You're a guy who likes to keep his options open. Understood."

I checked the clock. Twenty more minutes until this was over. I didn't want Zoe going nuclear in the car. With her temper, she was liable to grab the wheel and send us careening into oncoming traffic.

"I don't want to feel trapped like I did with Lena. I'm happy with the way things are. I want to go to the dance with you tomorrow and have a good time. I want to curse the gear shift in my car when I drop you off at your house tonight. I want you. Isn't that enough?"

She uncrossed her arms and laid her left hand on top of mine, which was resting on the gear shift. "You're right. I shouldn't care about labels."

"So we're good?"

...

Zoe

Hell no, we weren't good. Not like I'd tell him that. I wanted him to want to be my boyfriend. Did I want a promise of forever? No. But I wanted to know that he wasn't scanning the horizon for the next girl he would date.

I took a deep breath and lied. "Sure. We're good." Time to lighten the mood. "Did you see there's a Zombie Marathon on TV this weekend?"

"I think it's one of the laws of the universe that there's a Zombie marathon on some cable channel every weekend."

Not on the channels I had. "I guess, but it's still fun."

It was dark by the time we turned down the gravel road to my house. Grant turned his lights off and pulled into the deep shadows on the side of the driveway.

"Are you pretending you're in stealth mode? Because I guarantee everyone heard your car engine when we took the turn off for my house."

"Damn. I was being so sneaky."

"Who are you hiding from?" I asked.

"No one." He unbuckled his seatbelt, and I did the same. "Just hoping to hate the gearshift a little more."

My hormones went "Yippee" while my common sense frowned. Grant's lips pressed against mine, and I decided for now, common sense was overrated. The perverse part of my brain suggested I make him regret his non-boyfriend status a bit. Or maybe that was my hormones running the show. Either way, I threw myself into the moment.

When the kiss ended, I wasn't ready for him to leave. "If you're not ready to face your mom, you can hide out here for a while."

"That's not a bad idea."

"Cool." We climbed out of the car and headed into the house. My grandmother looked up from the living room where she sat crocheting.

"Hello, Grant. Avoiding your mother?"

I laughed at the surprised expression on Grant's face. "What can I say, we think alike." I tugged Grant toward the kitchen. "Let's grab a soda and walk to the pond."

"You have a pond?"

"Stocked with fish and skipping stones."

"Skipping stones. Are those like Mexican jumping beans?"

"Not at all." I grabbed two cans from the refrigerator. "There are picnic table cloths on top of the fridge if you want to grab one so we have something to sit on."

Grant reached up to grab a red and white checkered tablecloth.

Crash!

The distinct sound of metal crunching against metal came from the side of the house.

"What was that?" Grant jerked around and bam, his elbow smacked into my nose. I dropped the sodas and stumbled back a step. I saw stars. My eyes filled with tears, and I couldn't breathe.

"Shit, Zoe. Are you all right?" I gasped out a no.

...

Grant

"I'm so sorry."

"Mrs. Cain," I called out for Zoe's grandmother.

The front door flew open and Jack stormed in. "How could you be so stupid? Why would you park—"

"Shut up. Your sister is bleeding."

Her grandmother came rushing in. "What happened?"

"The sound of Jack hitting my car startled me and I accidentally elbowed Zoe in the face." I squatted down by her. "I am so sorry. Let me see." Zoe dropped her hands and what I saw punched me in the gut. Blood streamed from her nose down her chin. It looked like she was having trouble breathing.

"Breathe through your mouth," her brother said. "Here's a towel."

Her grandmother took the towel and held it under Zoe's nose. "I need to see if it's broken." She touched the bridge of Zoe's nose, making her wince. "I don't think it's broken. Grant, get a cold pack from the freezer."

I opened the freezer and grabbed one of those blue gel packs, which I handed to Zoe. "I am so sorry."

"It was an accident," Zoe mumbled through the towel.

"Yeah, well I still feel like a jerk."

"Take some Tylenol." Zoe's grandmother handed her the pills plus a glass of water. "At least it's the weekend. Most of the swelling should go down by Monday."

Zoe dropped the towel. "But the dance is tomorrow."

She looked like she was in a lot of pain and now she was upset about the stupid dance. How could I make this right?

"There's another dance at Christmas. We can go to that one."

"Okay." She held the ice to the bridge of her nose.

"Now that this situation is under control, let's go look at the cars," her grandmother said.

It didn't seem right to leave Zoe sitting here by herself. "Be right back."

On the way out the door, Jack started in again, "Zoe should have known better than to let you park in my spot."

"How could you not see my car?" I headed down the porch steps and rounded the corner of the house.

"Why would I look for a black sports car in the dark?"

"Boys, what's done is done. Let's assess the damage and contact your insurance companies."

Jack groaned. He was probably thinking about how much his insurance would go up. Then again, mine would probably go up, too.

The damage had sounded worse than it was. I'd need a new back bumper and tail lights. Jack would need new headlights and maybe a front bumper. The car was drivable so I wouldn't need a tow. After taking pictures of the damage, I used the insurance app on my phone and went back inside to check on Zoe.

She still looked like hell.

...

Zoe

It felt like someone had whacked me in the face with a frying pan, and I had to breathe through my mouth, but at least my nose had stopped bleeding. There was only one bright spot to this situation. Grant was more concerned about me than his car, which he loved. If I came before the car, that must mean he cared about me.

"Anything I can do?" Grant asked.

"What's going on here?" my mom called out, as she ran through the front door.

"Everyone is okay," my grandmother said.

My mom saw me through the kitchen doorway and rushed over. "Zoe? What happened?"

Grandma explained the situation.

"Come on, Zoe, I'll help you clean up and put on new clothes," my mom said. She pointed at Grant. "There's a bathroom down the hall you can use."

We went to the upstairs bathroom. My mom's hands shook as she helped me clean the blood off my face. "When I saw the cars out front—"

She must be thinking about when she'd seen the mass of tangled metal that had once been my dad's car. I grabbed her hand. "This hurts, but I'm okay."

"I know." She rinsed the bloody washcloth in warm water and went back to wiping off my face. "There. I think you're presentable for your boyfriend." She said the last part in a teasing tone."

I played along. "Shhhh, don't use that term. You might scare him away."

She leaned in and kissed me on the forehead. "I'm glad you're okay."

This was the most invested my mom had seemed in my life in a long time. While I wasn't happy to have an almost broken nose, having her pay attention to me again was nice.

Once I had on clean clothes, I brushed my teeth twice, which wasn't easy when I couldn't breathe through my nose. Part of me wanted to just lie down and go to bed, but another part of me wanted to go see Grant. When I made it back downstairs, he was sitting on the couch with his eyes closed.

When he heard me coming, he sat up and opened his eyes, and then he cringed. "I'm so sorry."

"I know. It was an accident. The Tylenol is kicking in, so it doesn't hurt as much."

"Good." He looked sort of lost. "Do you need anything?"

"Couch time with mindless television sounds good. You can stay if you want." I crossed the room and sat on the couch. He put his arm around my shoulders, and picked up the remote. "Mind if I drive?"

"No." I leaned into his warmth. My face had stopped throbbing, but I still had one hellacious headache.

He flipped through channels. "I always thought maybe I missed something by not having a brother or a sister, now I'm realizing that I'm better off as an only child."

"Jack can be a jerk, but he's basically a good guy."

Grant snorted like he didn't agree.

"What's the story behind your hate/hate relationship with my brother?"

"We competed against each other a lot. And then there was this girl, Katy, that I liked. Lena and I were on and off again, which should have been a clue. I met Katy when we were off, but she ended up dating your brother. We hung out, but then Lena and I got back together so nothing really happened."

"So, you never dated Katy?" That was different from the story my brother told me.

"Not really. The timing was off. And then she was with your brother and I was with Lena." Grant flipped through more channels, pausing on one of those shows where people hunt through old barns and find buried treasure. "These things have to be staged."

"Yeah, I know. If anyone went in the attic of our barn, all they'd find was dust and spiders."

"Maybe they're rare spiders worth a lot of money," he suggested.

"If you want to climb up there and see, be my guest."

"Maybe once you're better, we'll check it out together." His voice came right next to my ear. "You know, I've heard stories about barns with haylofts and adventurous farm girls."

Despite my injuries, his hot breath on my ear had my nerve endings in an uproar. "Do any of those stories mention that hay itches and it makes you sneeze?"

"And a perfectly good fantasy shot straight to hell."

I glanced sideways at him, his eyes were shining and he was grinning at me like there was no place else he'd rather be. My heart skipped a beat. "Thanks for staying here with me like this tonight."

Moving very slowly, he leaned down and pressed his lips to mine in a soft, sweet kiss. "It's the least I can do since my elbow tried to break your nose."

...

Grant

Zoe pressed her lips against mine one more time. Then she shifted around so she was facing the television and leaned back against me. We watched two guys dig through piles of junk stacked to the rafters of a barn.

When I'd seen blood running down her face earlier I'd felt like the biggest asshole on the planet. She'd been so brave about the whole thing. Lena would've demanded a plastic surgeon on the spot. Part of me still thought we should've gone to the hospital.

After the ice and the Tylenol, Zoe hadn't complained. I'd taken a punch to the nose before, and I knew it hurt. But she wasn't making a fuss. The thing she'd been the most upset about was the dance. So I'd jumped in and promised to take her to the next dance. Stupid maneuver.

Every time we established that we weren't boyfriend and girlfriend, something like this happened and screwed up the whole thing. I liked her, but I wasn't interested in any sort of commitment. And I knew that was what she was angling for. What I couldn't figure out was how I kept backing myself into this same corner.

"Why would anyone pay money for that?" Zoe asked.

On the television, a guy offered two hundred dollars for a pockmarked oil can sign. "You'd think the farmer would have to pay someone to take it. Not the other way around."

My cell rang, I checked caller ID. Great. "It's my father. I bet the insurance company called him." No putting this off. "Hello, father."

"Where are you? Are you all right?"

"I'm fine. Some idiot hit my car when it was parked." He didn't need to know the whole truth. Bringing Zoe into the situation would complicate the issue.

"Is this idiot related to the girl who keeps landing you in detention? Cain is a common last name, but I doubt it's a coincidence."

And my plan went out the window. "It's her brother. He has insurance. The car is drivable. It's not a big deal."

"Right. We'll discuss this when you come home." Click. He hung up on me.

"So now your dad loves me, too," Zoe muttered.

"At least we know my grandpa won't have a problem with you." I remembered something from earlier in the day. "Do you think your grandma is coming to dinner at my house Sunday?"

"If she said it, it's true." Zoe turned around, with an evil expression on her face. "You should record the whole thing on your phone so I can see how it turns out."

Right. "No deal. If I have to suffer through dinner, you're coming, too."

"Really?"

Damn. Damn. Damn. Damn. Damn. How did I keep screwing this up? How had I managed to invite Zoe to meet my parents? Apparently I was an idiot. I swear some higher power was messing with my head.

"No. Just joking. You're swollen nose gives you a pass."

"Oh." The sparkle left her eyes. She turned back around toward the TV.

And now I felt like a mean idiot. I needed to come up with a consolation prize to take her mind off my screw-up. "Want to go to the movies tomorrow, since we aren't going to the dance?"

"Maybe." She grabbed the remote and flipped channels until she landed on a zombie movie.

What did that mean? Was she imagining I was one of the zombies again, like at the arcade?

She put her hands in front of her eyes. "Tell me when the gross part is over."

"I didn't think you had a problem with Zombies dying."

"This is different. The video game is a cartoon. Cartoon brains, not gross. Special effects brains exploding, gross. I mean, just because some guy can make it look like the zombies guts are spilling all over the floor, doesn't mean I want to watch it."

"Then you probably shouldn't look now." One of the survivors hacked at the zombie with a tire iron. Not the best weapon of choice in a zombie war. "You can look now." She peeked between her fingers like a little kid. "Wuss."

"Hey." She elbowed me in the ribs. "No teasing the injured."

I wrapped my arms around her waist, blocking her from throwing any more elbows. She didn't even pretend to put up a fight.

"You're giving up awful easy."

She wiggled around a little bit until I could see her face. "I'm biding my time and plotting a sneak attack."

Right. "Let me know how that goes."

"Just wait." She faced the TV again. "You won't even see it coming."

Chapter Twenty-Two

Zoe

Twenty-four hours later, greenish yellow circles ringed my eyes. Not a flattering color for me. And my head ached enough that I was switching off between Tylenol and ibuprofen.

Delia sat across from me on my bed opening a bag of Hershey's kisses. She'd come over to assess the damage. "It's not that bad. I bet I could cover it with makeup. You could still go to the dance."

Should I tell Delia about Grant offering to take me to the Christmas dance when Delia hadn't been asked to this one? "If this annoys you, tell me to shut up."

"No problem." She unwrapped a kiss and popped one in her mouth.

"Grant said he'd take me to the Christmas dance instead."

She unwrapped two more kisses and shoved both of them in her mouth while she stared at the ceiling. Once she'd finished all three kisses, she unwrapped another. "He really came through for you in all this, didn't he? And yes there is a mild tone of irritation underlying that statement."

"I'm sorry for you, but happy for me. Even though Grant keeps yelling that he doesn't want a girlfriend, he stood by me, rather than worrying about his car."

"That's pretty awesome." Delia picked at a thread on my quilt. "Do you think Jack hit the car on purpose?"

"No. He griped about how much his insurance cost before the accident. I bet it goes way up after this."

"That's true," she said. "And it's not like he hit a normal car. Repairing the bumper on Grant's shiny little sports car won't be cheap."

"I kind of feel sorry for him."

My cell rang. Caller ID told me it was Grant. "Hey, Grant. What's up?"

"We may not be able to do the movies tonight."

Not what I wanted to hear. "Why not?"

"When my mom heard about the change in plans, she freaked out and said I had to attend the dance to pass the crown."

"If your mom likes Lena so much, let her go pass the stupid crown."

He laughed. "I suggested that. It didn't go over well."

"Where does that leave us?"

"I think I have to put in an appearance at the dance, but I don't have to stay."

"Is there a plan B? Because plan A sucks."

"You could come with me."

Could I go the way I looked? I wasn't sure. "My face...I have lemon lime colored rings around both my eyes."

"People will find out about the accident Monday, anyway. Does it matter if they see you now?"

"What's going on?" Delia asked.

I filled her in. "What do you think? Should I go?"

Delia walked toward my closet and pulled out the strapless black and white dress she'd made for me. "In this dress, people won't be focusing on your face."

I wasn't so sure. "Okay, Grant. Delia will help me with makeup and hair. I'll call you back with the results."

Thirty minutes later, I looked into the mirror and sighed. "From my chin down I rock." The green yellow rings around my eyes stood out underneath the makeup and my nose was lumpy and swollen.

"Your face isn't that bad," Delia said. Her tone was not convincing.

"Don't start lying to me now. I rely on your painfully honest opinion."

"Sorry. You must look better now than when Grant saw you right after the accident. To him this will be an improvement."

"Gee, thanks."

"What? You said be honest."

I called Grant and gave him the news. "You're going solo." He probably wouldn't be that way for long. "And since this was supposed to be our date, could you try not to pick up a girl while you're there?"

He laughed, but I wasn't kidding.

"I'll go to the dance, leave as soon as possible, and then I'll come see you. Deal?"

"Deal." I ended the call and flopped down on my bed. "I hate this."

"Everything will be fine. Since you aren't going out, let's practice making fancy cupcakes. When Grant comes over, I'll bail."

"Sounds good."

...

We baked a batch of vanilla cupcakes and then experimented with different colors of icing.

I made a giant pink flower on top of one cupcake. "What do you think?"

"I think it needs a little more sparkle." She grabbed the bottle of hot pink sugar crystals and sprinkled them on the flower.

Now it looked more like something from one of the high end bakeries. "Nice. I believe we have our contest entry. Let's make a dozen of them, and arrange them like a bouquet on green tissue paper. We'll call our entry, A dozen roses, aka I'm sorry I was an idiot, flowers."

Delia laughed. "I love it."

A few hours later when we were watching television, my phone buzzed. I grabbed it expecting to find a text from Grant. A photo of Grant kissing Lena on the dance floor smacked me in the face. Tears filled my eyes. How could he do that to me? I'd trusted him. "That son of a bitch."

"What?" Delia checked the phone. "Oh my God. I can't believe he'd do that."

I tossed my phone on the couch and focused on being angry. Angry was easier than sad. It took less of a toll.

Delia grabbed the phone and flipped through a few screens. "The picture came from a blocked number. I bet it's one of Lena's friends."

I took a step toward the shotguns hanging on the wall. In a perfect world, you'd be allowed to shoot people who cheated on you. And technically, I could shoot Grant, but the whole going to prison thing didn't sound like a good idea.

"Here." Delia handed me a throw pillow. "Go beat the crap out of the kitchen table."

"That's stupid."

"Pillow therapy is the reason I've never been to jail. Trust me."

I stalked into the kitchen, cleared off the kitchen table and whacked it with the pillow. Oddly satisfying. After hitting the table a dozen more times, I could breathe.

Delia made microwave popcorn, and then led me into the living room. She found a zombie movie. This time when the movie became gory, I didn't cover my eyes, I just imagined the zombies were Grant.

As the movie finished, someone knocked on my front door. I checked out the window and saw Grant. Red filled my vision, I yanked the door open. "What in the hell are you doing here?"

He looked confused. "I thought this was the plan."

"That plan went to hell when you kissed Lena."

"What are you talking about?"

"Catch." Delia threw my phone at him.

He caught it and looked at the picture. "Where did you get this?"

"Where? Why does that matter? What matters is you kissed her."

"Zoe, look at the picture." He shoved the phone toward me.

What did he think I was, some kind of masochist? "No thanks. I've seen it."

"No. You didn't. If you'd looked at it, you would have noticed something in the background." He enlarged the picture and pointed at a banner draped across a doorway.

It said Fall Dance, but it had last year's date. My brain tried to process this information. "This is last year's picture?"

"Yes."

A new wave of anger flowed through my veins. "That bitch. She set me up." I could feel Grant staring me down. "I'm sorry."

His disappointed expression didn't change. "Zoe, what's going on between us isn't working. Is it?"

The floor seemed to shift beneath my feet. The anger fled and in its place came a cold dull ache that radiated through my bones. He was breaking up with me.

I took a deep breath and blew it out slowly. "You're right. It's not. I can't do this anymore. You should go."

His eyes narrowed. "I didn't do anything wrong here."

"Not this time. But eventually, you will." And it would kill me. Not that this wasn't killing me. I clenched my hands into fists, driving my nails into my palms. This was the smart thing to do.

"Fine." He stormed off. I waited until I heard him drive away and then I let loose the tears.

...

My entire body ached, like I had the flu. I knew it was depression over Grant. How had I let myself fall for him, knowing the type of guy he was? It was like signing up to be someone's punching bag. How could I have been so stupid?

At school, it felt like I was moving in slow motion while everyone else buzzed about at their normal rate. I heard the term "ringer" a few times. Were they talking about me? Wouldn't that be freaking perfect?

I avoided the cafeteria, eating outside on one of the benches with Delia. "I don't think I can face him in Foods class."

She bumped me with her shoulder. "Don't forget, you'll have access to knives. That's a plus."

When the bell sounded to change classes, I headed for Foods, putting one foot in front of the other, not really wanting to reach my destination. Grant sat at our normal table. My only consolation? He looked like crap. Dark circles stood out under his eyes. Not that he met my gaze.

"Today, we begin our unit on cookies." Ms. Ida announced.

"Doesn't she make anything but desserts?" Grant mumbled.

I figured it was a rhetorical question, so I didn't bother answering.

Working in the tiny apartment-sized kitchen with Grant was torture. Before, I hadn't minded the close quarters. Brushing against each other was unavoidable at times. Each time our skin touched, there was a spark followed by a stab of emotional pain.

Did he feel the same way? Lips clamped together and eyes narrowed, he gave nothing away.

By the end of class I wanted to bolt from the room.

And that was my plan as soon as I finished cleaning up our kitchen.

"Can we talk?" Grant put away the last dry bowl.

"Here? No." Because I would get mad or sad or both and tears would come and I didn't need that embarrassment.

"Then where?" He stepped in front of me, blocking my path and preventing me from leaving the tiny kitchen.

And right on cue, my eyes started to burn. "Just call me tonight."

He didn't move. "I don't want to wait until tonight."

"Well, we can't always have what we want, can we?"

A muscle in his jaw ticked. "Stay after class and talk, or I'll dump over this canister of flour so you have to stay here and clean up with me."

There was a canister full of flour on the counter within arm's reach. "You wouldn't."

He smiled and smacked the canister onto the floor. A cloud of white dust rose into the air. "Oh no," he deadpanned. "Look what I've done."

"I can't believe you—"

"There's a broom and dustpan in the supply closet. You might need the mop, too," Ms. Ida called out. "Don't worry if you run late, I'll write you a pass."

"Thanks," I bit out.

The bell sounded, and our classmates filtered out of the room. Grant retrieved the broom. He swept while I held the dust pan.

"Now. You're going to listen to me. I'm not the bad guy here."

"I will attempt to ram this dustpan down your throat if you tell me that I can't be mad because we weren't exclusive."

He blinked. "Why am I bothering—"

"Good question." I took a dustpan full of flour and dumped it in the trash.

When I returned Grant pointed at me with the broom. "Shut up, and listen."

I wanted to yell, just because he told me to be quiet. But I didn't. "Fine. Talk."

"Before you went postal Friday night, I was going to tell you that the dance wasn't fun because you weren't there. Several other girls flirted with me and asked me to dance, and do you know what I did? I said no. Do you know why?"

I shook my head, afraid to say anything that would make him stop talking.

"All I could think about was leaving the stupid dance to see you."

Hope fluttered in my heart. "Really?"

"Yes. But once I got there you accused me of something I didn't do and then you broke up with me."

My world spun three hundred and sixty degrees. How had I gotten it so wrong?

"But...the only reason I broke up with you is because I didn't want to hear about how you could see other people if you wanted to."

"But that's not what I was going to say. If you'd given me a chance, instead of assuming you knew what I'd been about to say, we'd both be a lot happier right now."

Did that mean I'd lost my shot?

He just stared at me.

"You weren't trying to break up with me?" I gave a weak smile. "I'm sorry I thought you were."

"I wasn't." He continued sweeping. "If you'd trusted me, instead of believing I'd cheated on you, we wouldn't be in this situation."

"Right, because the twins at the Chinese restaurant didn't make you seem untrustworthy at all."

"Fine. Maybe I could have handled that differently, but you just believed that picture of me with Lena was real. You didn't even think about giving me the benefit of the doubt. You just believed the worst."

He was right. I had.

And I wasn't going to apologize again. I'd already done that. When the dustpan became full, I dumped it again. When he finished sweeping, he hung up the broom and exited the room. And I wanted to cry. Why hadn't I let him explain Saturday night? I'd just assumed he'd been about to break up with me, and kicked him off my porch. And now it was really over.

I checked the clock. No way would I make it to my next class on time. I walked up to Ms. Ida's desk.

She filled out a late pass and handed it to me. "Sometimes you don't get the ingredients right for a new recipe. That doesn't mean you shouldn't try it again."

I appreciated the encouragement, but I wasn't sure that her advice applied to this situation. Grant thought I didn't trust him, and the truth was, I hadn't, but maybe I should. How could I make him see that I was willing to trust him now?

All through classes, I thought about what I could say to Grant. Nothing I said would convince him that I trusted him. How could I show him? I spun my grandfather's watch around my wrist, and then I paused. The watch. Nothing I owned meant as much to me as this watch and he knew it.

At the end of the day, I knew what I had to do, so I rushed to the parking lot and waited for him by his car. When he saw me there, he frowned.

"This time, I was the one who messed up." Taking a deep breath, I unbuckled my grandfather's watch and showed him the inscription on the back. *Time isn't as important as the people you spend it with.* "To prove that I do trust you, I want you to have this." My hand shook as I held it out to him.

He didn't reach for the watch. "No. I can't take that. It means too much to you."

So did he. I needed him to see that. To see that I trusted him and I thought we were meant to be together. "I trust you to take care of it."

"Zoe—this isn't a good idea."

I swallowed over the lump in my throat. My resolve was fading. "I want you to have it." I shoved it at him.

He took it and strapped it around his left wrist. "Thank you." He didn't sound grateful. He sounded resigned. "I'll take good care of it."

I waited for him to say something else, but he just walked around me and opened his car door. My stomach hit the pavement. What had I expected?

...

Grant

Zoe's watch felt heavy on my wrist—probably because it came with some monster-sized emotional baggage. Why had she given it to me? A better question was why had I taken it? I'd tried not to, but there are only so many times you can say "no" without making a situation even more awkward.

Why couldn't things be simple? I remember my mother telling me someone like Lena would be an asset in my life. Not that I wanted Lena, but having someone who helped me, instead of making my life more difficult and confusing, would be a plus.

Maybe it was time to resort to Aiden's spreadsheet thought processes. On the positive side, Zoe was fun, and she made me smile. On the negative side, she was a drama queen who jumped to conclusions and threatened to shoot me on more than one occasion.

If I tried, I knew I could find another girl like Lena who wore the right clothes and came with the right social status. That would make my mother happy. Would it make me happy? I wasn't sure.

What would this new girl want from me? She wouldn't want me to take her to Edison's to shoot zombies or play air hockey. Then again, I could do those things with Aiden. If Zoe and I could get past this uncomfortable no-longer dating phase and become friends, we could still shoot zombies and eat pizza together. Was that what I wanted, to keep her as a friend?

By the time I pulled into the driveway I still didn't have a clue, but I didn't want to explain to my mother or father where the watch I was wearing came from so I took it off and slid it into my front pocket. Alone in my room, I took the watch out and read the inscription on the back.

Time isn't as important as the people you spend it with. Zoe's grandfather must have been a cool guy. Written on the face of the watch was the brand, Bulova. Curious, I Googled it. Similar watches were still being sold online at Amazon and in local jewelry stores for a couple of hundred dollars. The watch was worth way more than that to Zoe and I knew it, which was why I hadn't wanted to take it.

Now what? It ticked me off that Zoe had believed the worst about me, without even allowing me to explain. Then again, I had screwed up before. I set Zoe's watch on the desk next to the computer. She'd given it to me to show that she did trust me. It was a symbol. A peace offering which meant a lot to her.

Lena had never given me anything emotionally meaningful. Then again, I had chosen the earrings I gave her because they were the latest style and status symbol. They had meant nothing to me or to her. Now, that seemed shallow.

Zoe wasn't shallow. She tended to freak out first and ask questions later, which made her difficult, but when she realized she was wrong, she tried to make amends. Some people never admitted they were wrong. I imagined my life without her and it seemed a bit boring. Maybe we should give this relationship thing another try. We just needed to set some ground rules so we both knew where we stood.

I clicked on a link to a local jewelry store that sold and fixed watches.

Chapter Twenty-Three

Zoe

I saw Grant at school the next day, but he wasn't wearing my grandfather's watch. Had it meant so little to him? He'd said I could trust him with it. So even though it was killing me, I didn't ask. Maybe he was afraid to wear it. In Foods class, he made small talk like we were just friends. Is that what he wanted now? I wasn't sure I could just be his friend, because the first time I saw him kiss another girl I would more than likely cry or throw something at his head.

Wednesday at lunch, he and Aiden sat with us just like they had the day before. I watched as he squirted ketchup onto his fries in his preferred Spiderman style.

"You didn't ask me about your grandfather's watch yesterday."

"I didn't."

"Why not?" he asked.

How should I answer this question? I decided to go with painful honesty. "You know how much it means to me, and I trust you to keep it safe."

"Did you know that jewelry stores still make that kind of watch?" Grant asked.

Where was he going with this? "Sure, I mean, I guess I never thought about it."

"They also fix those kind of watches." He wiped his hands with a napkin, reached into his jacket pocket, and pulled out a small white paper bag.

"This is why I wasn't wearing it." From the bag he removed my grandfather's watch. Except it looked shinier than it had in a long time. The hole I'd punched into the leather using a nail had been cleaned up to look like a part of the watchband, and the hands on the watch were moving.

"You fixed it?" The watch hadn't worked in forever.

"I did." Grant placed it on my left wrist where he fastened it in place.

"Thank you." Not thinking, I leaned over and threw my arms around him in a hug. He hugged me back.

"You're welcome." He released me from the hug. "There's something else we should talk about."

I wasn't sure where this was going. It could be great, like he wanted us to get back together kind of great. Or, it could be awful as in the we're better off just being friends kind of talk which would result in me crying in the cafeteria in front of everyone.

"Maybe we should wait and talk in Foods." At least there the audience would be smaller.

"No. I think we need to do this here. What do you want, Zoe?"

I knew what I wanted...to be his girlfriend. Just him and me. No blondes—twins or otherwise—allowed. Is that what he wanted? I wasn't sure, but I did know that I didn't want to set myself up for humiliation in the cafeteria, so I turned the question back around on him. "What do you want?"

"I've spent a lot of time thinking about that lately." He paused and seemed to be waiting for me to volunteer something.

"You're dragging this out to torment me, aren't you?"

He leaned closer until we were nose to nose. "Zoe Cain, you are a foul tempered, evil girl, who shoots zombies for fun, but I like you and if you're interested, I want you to be my girlfriend."

I sucked in a breath, and then I kissed him. A happy sunshine warmth filled my body all the way down to my toes.

When we broke apart, it felt like I was floating.

"I'm guessing that was a yes." Grant said.

"It was." And then I saw the cafeteria monitor approaching. "Uh-oh."

When he was a few feet from the table he said, "You know what I'm going to say."

"Detention for both of us?" I asked.

He nodded and walked off.

"Is it me, or is detention starting to sound sort of romantic?" Grant asked.

He had a point. "I do sort of think of it as a package deal now, you know, detention and dinner."

"I never said anything about dinner," he teased, "and I hope you have a ride home."

"Don't worry. My boyfriend, will take care of me."

He gave a fake shudder. "You're a scary girl who uses scary words, but on that topic." He reached into his pocket and pulled out another white paper bag. "To keep your brother from being a jerk and to make sure that no one thinks you're the Ringer, I bought you this."

Not knowing what to expect, I reached into the bag and pulled out a silver charm bracelet. I recognized one charm as a heart, and then I laughed. "Is that a shotgun?"

"Yes." He fastened the bracelet around my right wrist and then pointed at each charm. "A cupcake for Foods, a pair of hedge clippers, since you like to threaten me with them, a zombie, a coffee cup, and this one."

I loved that he'd put so much thought into the charms. They were perfect. I leaned closer to read the flat circular charm. In tiny print, it said, "Girlfriend."

"Do you like it?" he asked.

"I love it."

"The saleslady at the jewelry store tried to steer me toward traditional girly hearts or red and pink crystals, but I knew that wasn't you."

...

On my way to the last class of the day, Amber approached me with a self-satisfied smile on her face. I braced myself for whatever dirt she was about to fling my way.

"After that display in the cafeteria today, I guess you and Grant are together now."

"We are."

"It looks like you get a tacky charm bracelet, and he wins the bet."

"First of all, it's not tacky, it's unique. Second, what bet are you talking about?"

"The Boyfriend Bet he made with Aiden. You didn't know about that?" She pretended to be shocked.

"No, but you obviously knew about it, or you wouldn't be enjoying this so much." I shifted my backpack higher on my shoulder.

"The day you told Lena that Grant was a dick and she could have him back, I told Grant what you said, and he bet Aiden that he could get you back if he wanted."

I dug my nails into my palm. "And you know this how?"

"After I told him about you, I sat at the table next to him. I guess he didn't realize I could still hear what he was saying. Go ahead and ask him if you don't believe me."

I was not going to play her game. "You know what, I believe you. That sounds exactly like something Grant and Aiden would do." And then I headed to class. My stomach churned as I turned this information over and over again in my brain. Should I be mad? Grant asking me to be his girlfriend didn't have anything to do with some stupid boyfriend bet. Grant and Aiden bet on things all the time but I hated that there was a tiny splinter of doubt in my mind.

I could text Grant and ask him about the bet, but that would make it look like I didn't trust him. And I did trust him. One thing I knew for sure...I needed to rein in my drama queen tendencies. Transforming into a jealous, controlling girlfriend was the surest way to screw up this brand new relationship. I decided to go with slightly insecure, possibly plotting to slash his tires if he dumps me after winning the money type of girlfriend, instead.

After class ended, I headed to detention. What should I say to Grant? Should I ask about the bet? Knowing Amber, she'd probably already told the entire school about it, so I'd just play it cool and wait for him to bring it up. If he didn't mention it, I wouldn't either.

Grant pacing outside the office door showed he was worried about my reaction.

"Nervous about detention?" I asked. "Because I'm pretty sure we know how to do this."

He studied me. "You're not mad?"

"About?" Okay I knew he was talking about the bet, but I wanted to see how much he was going to admit.

"Amber texted me that she told you about a bet Aiden and I made."

"The Boyfriend Bet? Yes, she mentioned that." I shrugged. "You guys bet all the time. I don't think that's the reason we're together now. Is it?"

"No. It's not." He exhaled like he'd been holding his breath and now he could relax. "Thanks for not freaking out."

"I am trying to tone down my drama queen ways." Grant may not be perfect, but he wouldn't do anything to hurt me on purpose. I knew he wasn't trying to make me the Ringer. I didn't know how this relationship would end up, but I guess that's how all relationships start out…taking a leap of faith and trusting that the other person cares for you.

…

That night while I sat crocheting in the living room with my grandma and my mom, I showed them my bracelet and told them the happy news.

"Thank goodness," my grandmother said. "Now I can see Everett again."

I held up the scarf and eyed the previous row, checking to see if it was even. "You wouldn't go out with him because of me?"

"Of course not." Light flashed off her pink metallic crochet hook as she worked on her latest afghan. "I couldn't spend time with a man whose grandson hurt my granddaughter."

"Thank you. I guess now you can go have dinner with his lovely daughter-in-law."

"No way. I'm insisting we go out to eat."

…

Grant

I hadn't planned on mentioning the fact that I'd asked Zoe to be my girlfriend, but my grandfather outed me at dinner by saying, "I heard you worked things out with Monica's granddaughter."

"I did."

"Maybe you two should go on a double date," my dad said from behind his tablet.

"That has bad idea written all over it." I glanced toward my mother's vacant chair. "And we probably shouldn't mention any of this to Mom."

My grandfather chuckled. "I heard about the scene at school. Even when she was a girl, Monica was not one to keep her opinions to herself."

My dad set his tablet down. "Your mother told me about what happened that day, how she insisted Zoe be kicked out of school and honestly, I don't think it's that she dislikes Zoe."

"Really, because that's exactly what it looked like."

"I think your mom liked seeing you with Lena because she and Lena have similar personalities. She thought Lena would take care of you the way she's always taken care of me."

Huh. "Maybe that's true but the last time we talked about this, you seemed to resent how she handled you."

"I thought I resented her for hovering over me. When she backed off, I missed having her around."

My mother entered the dining room with a smile on her face. "Missed having who around?"

"You." My dad smiled at her, and his emotions seemed genuine.

She blushed. "Thank you."

Should I confess my relationship with Zoe and risk ruining the first harmonious family dinner we'd had in ages?

"It's nice to see you two happy around each other again," my grandfather said. "Every marriage goes through rough spots. The key is to hold on to the people who make your life fun."

"I think you're right." She sat and took a sip of her wine. "And I might have been wrong about something else. Grant, does this Zoe girl you've been seeing make you happy?"

"Yes."

"Then I'll give her a chance."

"Thank you." It felt like the last piece of the puzzle had fallen into place. Zoe made my life fun. I didn't know what would happen long term, but for now, she made me happy. The one thing that would make the situation better is if I could get Aiden on board with Delia. I bet if Zoe and I put our heads together we could make it happen.

...

Zoe

I held my breath as the bake sale auctioneer announced our entry. "Here we have a dozen edible cupcake roses, also known as, I'm sorry I was an idiot flowers." She laughed. "Men, take note. This is something you could all use from time to time."

"What if no one bids?" I whispered to Grant.

"Don't worry, I've got it covered."

"How?"

"I asked my grandfather to bid on it."

"Thank you."

"We'll start the bidding at ten dollars," the auctioneer announced. People around us held up their numbered paper paddles. The auctioneer went so fast,

I wasn't sure what the final bid was, but it was more than a hundred dollars. It might not have been the highest price of the evening, but it was in the top half.

"Thank goodness that's over," I said. "Now I can finally relax."

"Hello, Grant." I heard two feminine voices say in unison.

We turned to see who was talking. The tall, tan, blonde twins from the Chinese restaurant were back. Fabulous. A tingle of insecurity trickled down my spine.

"Hello, Georgette, Angeline. I believe you've met my girlfriend, Zoe."

"That's right, "Georgette said with her fake smile on high-beam. "Hello."

"Hello, nice to see you again," I lied through my teeth.

Angeline's smile was a little weak as she nodded at me. "Nice to see you, too."

I smiled and nodded as they talked with Grant about places I'd never been and would probably never go.

By the time they walked away, my face hurt.

Grant looked at me like he expected me to say something.

"What?" I asked.

"Better than the Chinese restaurant?"

"Much better. Thank you."

"Maybe I should write a guide on how to be a good boyfriend."

I laughed. "Seriously?"

"I aced that situation, thank you very much."

"You're right. You did. So what would you call this guide?"

He squinted like he was thinking. "What about the
Boyfriend Book, or The Best Boyfriend."

"Or, How to Be the Best Boyfriend You Can Be."

"Too wordy," he said. "Wouldn't look good on a book cover."

"True." I thought about it. "You know, it's not such a ridiculous idea."

"There you are," a woman said from behind us. I turned to see Grant's mother, wearing a polite, if somewhat strained, smile.

"Hello, Mother. I'm sure you remember Zoe."

"I do." She nodded at me.

"Hello." I had no idea what else to say.

"You seem to make my son happy."

Why did it feel like I was walking into a trap? "He makes me happy, too."

"I think we started off on the wrong foot. If you could avoid landing Grant in detention, I'm willing to start over."

"Okay." I glanced at Grant. "But it's not always my fault."

Grant laughed. "We will make a sincere effort to avoid detention."

"Good. Now I better go see what your father is up to. He thinks he wants to bid on a box of smelly cigars. Can you imagine?" And she walked off.

That was a little odd, but one fact stood out. "Your mom doesn't hate me."

"Now the only person left to convert is your brother," Grant said.

"I wouldn't hold my breath on that one." Not that it mattered.

Another auction started. It was for a set of paints Delia would love. I scanned the crowd for her and saw her next to my brother, which was weird. And she was bidding on the paints.

"Look over there." Grant pointed to Aiden who was on the other side of the room holding up his paddle. "He doesn't paint."

"Maybe he's buying them for Delia?" I really wanted them to get together. "Has he said anything to you about her?"

"He thinks they're good as friends, for now," Grant said.

"I bet we could get them together, if we tried."

"Agreed. Now all we need is a plan."

We put out heads together and talked about different scenarios we could set up to encourage our best friends to date. It was funny that Grant was all for getting his best friend a girlfriend when he'd sworn not so long ago that was something he himself didn't want.

"What are you smiling about?" he asked.

"You, us, the plot to make our best friends happy."

"We do have a lot to celebrate." He glanced around. "There are teachers from Wilton here, and technically it's a school event, but I'm willing to risk it."

"Risk what?"

"This." And he leaned down and kissed me. Sliding my arms up his chest to his shoulders felt just as natural as it had the first time I'd kissed him. Funny that it was Jack, my temper, and my drama queen ways that had brought us together. Whatever the circumstances, the bet, or my interfering brother, we fit together perfectly. Only time would tell how long it would last. But I planned to enjoy every minute of it.

Acknowledgments

It takes a lot of people to bring a book to life. I'd like to thank Erin Molta and Stacy Abrams for editing my Boyfriends into shape. I'd like to thank my family for all their encouragement and support.

About the Author

Award winning author Chris Cannon lives in Southern Illinois with her husband and various furry beasts. She believes coffee is the Elixir of Life. Most evenings after work, you can find her caffeinating and writing fire-breathing paranormal adventures, paranormal cozy mysteries, or sweet snarky romances. You can find her online at www.chriscannonauthor.com.

Also by Chris Cannon

Going Down In Flames
Bridges Burned
Trial By Fire
Fanning The Flames
Burning Bright

Mysteries of Mystic Hills
Murder in Mystic Hills
Double Trouble in Mystic Hills
SpellBound in Mystic Hills

Sweet Snarky Romance Series
The Boyfriend Bet

Watch for more at https://www.chriscannonauthor.com/.

www.ingramcontent.com/pod-product-compliance
Lightning Source LLC
Chambersburg PA
CBHW020424180626
46812CB00003B/1132